8   DINOS

MW00961902

The Raptor's Claw

To Murray, with memories of the museum .—BBC

For Thomas O'Leary Jr.—D O'L

8 DINOSAUR DETECTIVE
The Raptor's Claw

FOOTHILLS ACADEMY

B. B. Calhoun

illustrated by Danny O'Leary

Scientific
American
BOOKS FOR YOUNG READERS

W. H. FREEMAN AND COMPANY ◆ NEW YORK

Book design by Debora S. Smith

Scientific American Books for Young Readers is an imprint of
W. H. Freeman and Company, 41 Madison Avenue
New York, New York 10010

This book was reviewed for scientific accuracy by Don Lessem, founder of The Dinosaur Society.

Library of Congress Cataloging-in-Publication Data

Calhoun, B. B., 1961–

The raptors claw/ B. B. Calhoun [i.e. Christina Lowenstein] ; illustrated by Danny O'Leary.

—(Dinosaur detective ; #8)

Summary: While with his father on a trip to the natural history museum in New York, Fenton solves the mystery surrounding the old paleontologist in the attic.

ISBN 0-7167-6606-X (hc). —ISBN 0-7167-6607-8 (pb)

[1. Museums—Fiction. 2. Paleontology—Fiction. 3. Mystery and detective stories.] I. O'Leary, Danny, ill. II. Title. III. Series: Lowenstein, Christina. Dinosaur Detective ; #8.

PZ7.C12744Rap1995

[Fic]—dc20   95-11467
                                                CIP
                                                AC

Printed in the United States of America.
10 9 8 7 6 5 4 3 2 1

1

"Wow," said Willy Whitefox, "a belt with a dinosaur on it."

"My mom just sent it. It's an early Christmas present," Fenton Rumplemayer explained to his friend. He rolled up the belt, which had a head-on view of a tyrannosaurus on the buckle, and put it on his bed next to the other clothes he was packing.

Fenton still couldn't believe that the next morning he and his father would get on a plane for New York City. It would be the first time they'd been back to New York since they'd moved to Morgan, Wyoming, the summer before. Mr. Rumplemayer, who was a paleontologist, had been sent to Morgan by the New York Museum of Natural History to head a dig team looking for dinosaur fossils. But recently the museum had asked Fenton's father to come back for a few days to help supervise the opening of their brand-new Mesozoic Hall, which would feature fossils and reconstructions of dinosaurs and other Mesozoic animals. Since Fenton was off from school for winter vacation, they'd decided to spend Christmas in New York.

Fenton picked up the belt and slipped it into the bag, wondering how his mother was going to spend Christmas this year. Mrs. Rumplemayer was also a paleontologist and had been given a grant to study dinosaurs in India. Fenton wasn't too sure they even had Christmas in India.

It definitely wasn't going to be like the Christmases they had all been together, thought Fenton. He dug into a drawer and took out a heavy wool sweater.

"Is it cold in New York?" asked Willy. He squeezed onto the one corner of Fenton's bed not covered by the travel bag and things being packed.

"Yeah, sometimes it's pretty chilly," said Fenton, remembering how the wind came whistling between the tall buildings. "But they don't have nearly as much snow as we get here."

"It's bye-bye snow for me," said Willy, leaning back and putting his hands behind his head. "I can't wait to get to Hawaii—surfing and skin-diving. I bet I'm the luckiest kid in Morgan."

"No way," said Fenton. "What's the big deal about sun? I'm going to hang out at the museum every single day."

Fenton had grown up across the street from the New York Museum of Natural History. Both his parents had worked there, and from the time he was really little, Fenton had spent most of his free time with the dinosaur skeletons, studying and sketching them. He was looking forward to seeing the museum again—and to seeing his friend Max, too. Max lived in Fenton's old building in New York, and they had been in the same class at school.

Just then there was a loud thump as something hit the outside of the attic wall next to Fenton's window. Willy sat up.

Fenton peered through the frost-covered window. He pushed the window open. In the yard stood his friend Maggie Carr, winding up to throw a second snowball.

"Watch out! This one's coming right in," she called.

6

Fenton put his hands up just in time. The powdery snow splashed all over his flannel shirt and into the room.

"Okay, truce," he yelled. "We don't have any ammo up here! Come on up."

Maggie laughed and bounded toward Fenton's back door.

"I wonder what Maggie's going to do for two weeks of vacation without us around," said Fenton.

"Oh, she'll probably spend all her time riding," said Willy.

Maggie lived on a horse ranch. She'd been riding since she was little, and she even had her own horse.

"Hi, guys," said Maggie, popping through the hole in the floor where the ladder came up to the attic.

"Hi, Maggie," said Fenton. He zipped up his travel bag and eased it onto the floor.

Maggie took off her parka. "Hey, listen, Connecticut's pretty close to New York, right?"

"Uh huh," said Fenton. "Some parts of it. One of the kids in my old school actually *lived* in Connecticut. Why?"

"Oh, no reason," said Maggie. "It's just, you know my mother went to that snooty Yardley University there, right?"

"Has she gotten over the way we beat them in the McAlpin competition yet?" asked Fenton. Fenton and Willy had recently helped Fenton's father's dig team win a paleontological contest that had pitted them against Yardley.

"Oh, she's decided it was a fluke. She's still set on getting Lila to go to college there," said Maggie. Lila was Maggie's older sister. "Of course, Lila wants to go to Wyoming State, to be near her boyfriend. Anyway, my mother's making Lila go for an interview at Yardley just before their Christmas break. She's supposed to stay with Great-Aunt Margaret in Connecticut for the holidays."

"So you're getting rid of Lila for a while, huh? That's a pretty good Christmas present," joked Fenton. Maggie and her older sister didn't get along very well.

Maggie sighed dramatically. "Actually, my parents are going on a trip too. They decided to take a vacation in Mexico." She grinned. "And, I'm going to Connecticut, too! Which means I'll even be able to come to New York to do my Christmas shopping!"

"You're really going to be in Connecticut?" said Fenton in amazement.

"That's right," said Maggie happily. "We leave in a few days." She made a face. "The only bad part is I have to spend my whole vacation with Lila. Ugh!"

Fenton grinned. This was great news. If Maggie came to visit New York, he'd be able to show her the museum and everything.

The following afternoon, the Rumplemayers' taxi turned down a New York City street and pulled up in front of a three-story brownstone house. The owners of the house, the Palmers, were away. Mrs. Palmer worked at the museum and had agreed to have Fenton and his father house-sit while they were away.

While his father paid the driver, Fenton pulled their bags and his stegosaurus backpack out of the cab. He looked up at the brownstone. It was kind of strange to think of staying in a real house right in the middle of New York City. Most people in this part of the city lived in tall apartment buildings, as the Rumplemayers had before they'd moved.

9

Fenton and his father went inside, put down their luggage, and took off their coats in an entry area just inside the front door. To their right was a wooden staircase, and in front of them was a large living room with an old brick fireplace. Beyond it Fenton could see a large dining room and kitchen.

"Wow, this place is neat," said Fenton, looking around.

"Yes, very nice," agreed his father. He reached for a phone on a table next to the stairs. "I've got to check in with the museum. Why don't you just grab a bedroom upstairs, son."

Fenton headed up. On the floor above the living room he found three bedrooms. On the top floor he found two more rooms. One looked like a study, or an office of some kind, and the other was a bedroom, with an old-fashioned model airplane hanging from the ceiling and some New York Mets posters tacked up on the walls.

Putting his bag and backpack down, he sat on the bed and bounced once. I'll take it, he thought.

He looked out the window. He could see empty yards and the backs of other row houses like the one he was in. Then he recognized, just past them, the top of a wall with a slanted gray roof above it. The museum!

"Fenton!" his father called up the stairs.

Fenton went to the door. "Up here, Dad," he answered.

"I'm going over to the museum," his father said. "Do you want to come along?"

Fenton looked back into the bedroom. The clock on the windowsill said two-thirty. Max's school didn't begin its vacation until the next day so he wouldn't be home for an hour.

"Sure, Dad. Be right there."

A few minutes later, with his sketch pad in his backpack, Fenton walked beside his father toward the museum.

This was going to be a great vacation, thought Fenton. He'd be able to spend a ton of time at the museum, hang out with Max, and see Maggie, too. He had nothing else to do for two weeks.

Well, almost nothing, he reminded himself. There was that history report he still had to write. The rest of his class had finished it while Fenton and his father had gone to Hollywood for a week to work on a dinosaur movie. He would have to squeeze that in somewhere. The assignment was to investigate the history of something that existed today. The hardest part was getting started. If only there were some way he could do his report on dinosaurs. But there weren't exactly any dinosaurs around today.

They turned a corner and Fenton saw the museum. The building, which took up three city blocks, had a big arched entryway at its center. Fenton always thought that it looked like a castle from the outside, especially at the four corners, which were round turrets with pointy roofs.

They headed toward the main entrance, passing the small, old-fashioned guard booth on the way. Across the street Fenton could see the coffee shop where he and Max sometimes stopped for sodas after school. Fenton felt a surge of excitement. He wondered what the new Mesozoic Hall would look like.

Minutes later he and his father were walking through the large entry hall of the museum and past the big marble stairs.

"Are you going to the new exhibit hall?" said Fenton. He wasn't even sure where it was.

"I certainly am, Fenton," said his father. "It's right this way."

They rounded a corner and found that the hallway was blocked by a plywood wall with a small door in it. On the wall was a sign that read PARDON OUR APPEARANCE, and below it a smaller one saying AUTHORIZED PERSONS ONLY.

Mr. Rumplemayer opened the door, and they went in. The new exhibit hall was a lot bigger than any of the older galleries, and Fenton soon realized it had been made by building a skylight over one of the museum's courtyards.

"Wow!" said Fenton. "Look at that!" Rearing up in front of him was a huge dinosaur skeleton. Fenton was amazed at the towering, carefully balanced pose it had been set in—and its sheer size. "What is it, Dad, a diplodocus?" he asked.

"Right, son," said his father. "And pretty impressive, too."

There was a scaffold next to the dinosaur's neck, which hadn't been finished yet. A man and a woman stood on the scaffold, adjusting a vertebra. This was great, thought Fenton. He'd be able to see how a huge dinosaur skeleton was actually assembled. He opened his stegosaurus backpack and took out his sketchbook.

"I guess I should find Ms. Soames, the museum director," said Mr. Rumplemayer. "She promised to arrange a temporary office for me while we're here. I want to find out where it is."

Fenton remembered Ms. Soames. He had met the museum director a few times, and she had always been friendly to him.

"I think I'll just stay here and draw this new exhibit, Dad," said Fenton.

"Fine, son," said his father. "I'll see you later. You can come find me here, or we'll just meet back at the house."

Fenton sat down on the floor and started to sketch the diplodocus. A few minutes later, he saw the man and the woman on the scaffold lift the next neck bone into place. Surprisingly, they seemed to do it with practically no effort. Fenton shook his head in amazement. Fossilized bones were usually pretty heavy. It didn't make sense that this bone could be lifted so easily. He stood up, deciding to ask the man and the woman about it.

But just then a man Fenton had never seen before came striding across the room toward him. He was dressed in a shiny blue suit, and his face was bright red As the man got closer, Fenton could see that he looked angry. His red Adam's apple was fluttering up and down on his red neck. Even the top of his head was red, except for several strands of black hair.

"*You!*" said the man, shaking a red finger at Fenton. "You are an unsupervised minor in an area of the museum closed to the public. Hence, you are in very serious trouble."

Fenton gaped at the man in astonishment. Nothing like this had ever happened to him before. He'd always been able to go anyplace he wanted in the museum.

"B-but my father brought me here," he managed to say.

The man opened a small two-way radio.

"This is Smythe," he said into it. "I want a security guard in the new exhibit area on the double. Is that clear?"

Oh no, thought Fenton, this was terrible. His first time back at the museum and he was in trouble. Why hadn't his father told him he wasn't allowed there? He swallowed and took a deep breath.

"My father's Bill Rumplemayer," he tried. "He works here."

"Rumplemayer? Works here?" said the man. "There's no one by that name on the staff, so don't make it worse by making up stories." He looked over Fenton's shoulder. "Ah, security."

"Yes, Mr. Smythe," said a voice from behind Fenton.

"Security, this boy is an unsupervised minor in an unauthorized area. I want him arrested for trespassing, or whatever it is we do in these cases."

The guard moved around to Fenton's side.

"Well, we don't necessarily go through all that on a first offense, Mr. Smythe. We—" He stopped suddenly and looked at Fenton. "Why, Fenton, how are you doing?"

"Hi, Jeff," said Fenton in relief. Jeff Masters was a paleontology student who'd worked part-time as a guard at the museum for three years. He'd always been interested in Fenton's drawings.

"I believe this trespasser's father works in the Paleontology Department, Mr. Smythe," he said. "Mr. Rumplemayer's been in the field since last summer. This is Fenton Rumplemayer. He's been roaming around the museum for years."

"He has, has he?" said Mr. Smythe, obviously displeased. "Well, I'm going to have to see the director about this. We can't have unauthorized minors wandering around causing trouble."

"I wasn't trying to cause trouble; I was just sketching the display," said Fenton.

"You see that?" said Mr. Smythe. "He admits it! This display is going to be unveiled at the annual Christmas party. No unauthorized photographs or sketches are permitted until then." He turned to Jeff. "Security, confiscate that sketchbook."

14

Jeff rolled his eyes a bit as he held his hand out for Fenton's sketchbook. Luckily, Mr. Smythe didn't catch Jeff's expression.

"And make sure you take this *child* to one of the public areas of the museum," Mr. Smythe finished as he marched off.

"I see you've met our new director of security," Jeff said with a sigh. As they walked together to one of the open galleries, he opened Fenton's sketchbook and began looking through it. "These are great, Fenton. But I guess I'd better 'borrow' this one of the diplodocus till after the opening party. If Mr. Smythe finds you with it, there's going to be one *dino*-mite explosion."

Fenton laughed. As long as he could remember, Jeff had been making up dinosaur jokes like that. He sometimes called himself a *tricera*-cop.

"Okay," said Fenton. He took the sketchbook and tore out the drawing. "Hey, thanks for getting me out of that, Jeff."

"No problem," said Jeff, taking the drawing from him. "Now enjoy the museum. Sometimes I think Mr. Smythe forgets that's what it's here for."

As Fenton made his way through the museum, visiting some of the older dinosaur halls and checking out some new exhibits, he put his run-in with Mr. Smythe out of his mind.

He found a new kentrosaurus skeleton and sat down in front of it to make some sketches. He carefully drew its plates and spikes, and, noting the metal frame and little rods that held the pieces together, he decided to include them in his drawing too.

As he drew, Fenton began to imagine himself as a paleontologist who assembled dinosaur fossils for display. He was a grown-up, of course—the world's leading expert in dinosaur

15

reconstruction. He had pioneered new methods that gave his dinosaurs such a lifelike look that museum visitors would have to look twice to be sure that the dinosaur bones hadn't come back to life. Just then, the museum's lights began to blink, signaling closing time.

Fenton sighed and closed his pad. He thought of going to look for his father, but remembering Mr. Smythe, he decided not to. Instead, he made sure he was out the main entry door before it was locked.

Fenton crossed the street and walked past the coffee shop. It felt great to be back at the museum. It had been exciting to see his favorite old dinosaur skeletons as well as the new finds, like the kentrosaurus, that the museum had added to its collection since he had been gone. Then Fenton had an idea. Maybe he should write his history report about the museum. He could probably even use the museum's own library to find out more about the early days, when it had first been founded. It was a great idea, he decided. In fact, it was the next-best thing to writing about dinosaurs themselves.

Fenton turned to look back at the looming stone building with its four corner turrets. The visitor lights were out, and he could make out the silhouettes of a few skeletons through the windows of the main floor. He thought again of how much the big old building looked like a castle or a fortress.

Then Fenton noticed something else, something very peculiar. Coming from one of the small windows in the slate-covered attic was a solitary light. That's strange, he thought. The museum was closed. Why would a light be on way up there in the attic?

2

"Okay, how about this?" said Fenton. He was talking to his friend Max on the phone on his second day in New York. "First we'll play Treasure Quest, and then we can go to the museum."

Max, who was a computer genius, had invented a computer game called Treasure Quest. Back when Fenton had lived in New York, the two boys had played all the time. They had even managed to play once a week since Fenton had moved to Wyoming, by hooking up their computers through modems.

"But I was just in the museum when my cousins were here for Thanksgiving," said Max.

There was a beep as Fenton's phone signaled that another call was coming in.

"Hang on a second," he said. He clicked the receiver. "Hello?"

"Hi, Fen, it's Maggie. I'm at my aunt Margaret's."

"Hi," said Fenton. "How's it going? Are you going to come into New York?"

"I'm sure I'll be able to in a few days," said Maggie.

"Today's Tuesday, right?" With no school, Fenton had lost track of time. "How about Saturday?"

"The day before Christmas Eve," said Maggie. "Okay. I can still do some shopping. Hang on, I'll ask Aunt Margaret."

"Okay, I'll finish up with Max on the other line," said Fenton.

He clicked the receiver. "Hi, Max," he said. "That was Maggie. She's going to try to come in on Saturday. About today, my father told me they're adding a new computer center to the museum's library. I have to go there for my history report anyway."

"I didn't see a computer center there," said Max.

"It's not really open yet," said Fenton. "It's part of the renovation work." Then he remembered Mr. Smythe and being an unauthorized minor. "We're going to have to look out for this guy who threw me out of a closed area, though. Hold on, let me see if Maggie's back." He clicked again. "Maggie?" he said.

"Yeah, I'm here," said Maggie. "She said it's okay. I'll call you Friday, and we can figure out exactly what we're doing."

"Great," said Fenton. "Talk to you then." He clicked the receiver once more. "So what do you think, Max?" he asked.

"If there are new computers there, I'm in," said Max. "But I have to be home early. Hanukkah starts tonight."

"No problem," said Fenton. "Hey, do you want to come over here and see this place today? My father's laptop is here."

"I guess we could play Treasure Quest on the laptop," said Max. "Okay, I'll bring over the disk."

Later that afternoon, after playing several games of Treasure Quest, Max and Fenton walked over to the museum.

"The library's on the fourth floor," said Fenton, starting up the grand staircase. Their sneakers squeaked on the marble stairs as they raced each other up. "This way." Fenton pointed to a corridor to the right of the stairs.

But then they encountered a plywood wall like the one Fenton had seen outside the new gallery the day before. A sign said PAR-

DON OUR APPEARANCE on it, too, but there was no door.

"I guess we should try going around the other way," said Fenton. He knew the museum was shaped like a giant squared-off 8, with the library located in one of the corner turrets. They went back to the central stairs and started down a smaller corridor. "If you see a tall bald guy, we'd better take off," said Fenton. "He's really strict about who's allowed where."

They made their way through the dimly lighted corridor.

"Hey, look at that big elevator full of stuffed raccoons," said Max. They passed the ancient elevator cab, which Fenton had often seen parked in a cluttered storage room on the first floor. Soon they came to another plywood barrier and then to an unfinished area under a sloped roof.

"We must be in the part of the fourth floor that's an attic," said Fenton. They followed a string of construction lights until a turn in the plywood wall led them to a new, even smaller corridor. Fenton felt a cobweb brush his face.

"Do you still know where you're going?" asked Max.

"Actually, I don't think I've ever been in this part of the museum before," Fenton admitted. He stopped and peered ahead. Then he noticed a light under a door along the corridor wall. "Look," he said. "Let's see if there's anyone in there."

"I hope it isn't that guy's office you were telling me about," whispered Max.

"Mr. Smythe? I don't think so." Fenton tapped on the door, and they heard rustling inside. Then the door swung slowly open.

The room was tiny, with a sloped ceiling. The walls were covered with shelves that were crammed with pieces of bones, small dinosaur skulls, and skeletons. Stacks of papers filled the room's corners, and there were little saws, drills, and other tools mounted on one wall. Wedged beside the door was a desk with a single bright lamp shining on it. Hunched over the desk was an old man with a giant magnifying glass.

"And what brings you boys to this lonely corner of the museum?" asked the man. He had tufts of white hair and wore an old-fashioned shirt with no collar.

"W-we were looking for the library," Fenton stammered.

"And the new computer center," added Max.

"Well, you've found Mr. Binks's office," said the old man. "The office of unsolvable reconstruction problems."

Reconstruction, Fenton knew, meant putting fossil skeletons together as they had been before a dinosaur or some other animal had died. Fenton gazed around at the collection of carefully assembled fossils that lined the office's shelves. He pointed to a small, birdlike skeleton on a shelf above the work table. "Was the reconstruction of that compsognathus done by Mr. Binks?"

"Oh, I see you know your dinosaurs, my friend," said the old man. He smiled, but as he did, Fenton noticed that his eyes weren't smiling. They looked a little sad. "Yes," the man continued, "Binks put that fellow together."

Fenton was impressed. The compsognathus was mounted in a running pose, leaning forward, its right foot poised in the air and its long tail extended behind it. The animal really looked as if it were about to run across the room. It couldn't have been easy to assemble all those tiny bones so flawlessly.

"It's great," he said sincerely. He glanced again at the small

21

instruments on the wall. "And those are some nice tools you have there—er, Mr. Binks has."

"I guess I'll admit to being Binks," said the old man with a laugh, "since I'm dealing with someone who knows his fossils. Yes, this is a good set of tools. I got that drill at the end of the war. Army-surplus dental equipment. You could get it for a song."

"Is that how you attach the bones together?" asked Max.

"Sometimes," answered Mr. Binks. "Drill holes and then set a pin. Or you can use a steel frame, an armature. Whatever works." He pointed to the compsognathus. "'Course, in these little ones you have to use very small holes. Otherwise there's nothing left."

"I guess the hard part must be getting the whole thing to stand up," said Fenton, looking again at the skeleton with admiration. "Fossils can be pretty heavy."

"Used to be," said the old man. "Nowadays they're not using the original fossils for the big exhibits. Plastics, don't you know. They make lightweight plastic copies of each bone. Much easier to have a big diplodocus stand on its hind legs that way. They say it's more dramatic. But me, I never met a piece of plastic I liked."

Fenton thought of the workers he'd seen lifting the vertebra so effortlessly in the new exhibit hall. The new diplodocus must be made of plastic. It was probably a lot easier to work with plastic bones than real ones, Fenton reflected. But Mr. Binks seemed to prefer the real thing. And judging from the beautiful specimens in his office, the old man must be something of an expert.

Then Fenton remembered why they'd come to the museum in the first place. "Mr. Binks, could you tell us how to get to the library? I've been there before, but there's a construction barrier across the hall there now."

"Why sure, boys," said Mr. Binks. "Just before you get to the barrier, there's a door in the corridor painted red. That's going to be the new entrance. There's no sign yet."

"Thanks," said Fenton. "And thanks for showing us all this great stuff, too."

"Well, I'm glad you stopped in," said Mr. Binks. "Sometimes I start to feel lost up here."

Soon the two boys were walking by the elevator again.

"Wow, that was cool," said Fenton. "Did you see some of those things he put together? He must be one of the most talented dinosaur reconstructors the museum has. There was just one thing I didn't understand."

"What's that?" asked Max.

"Why would such an incredible dinosaur builder be hidden away in that back corner of the attic?"

3

Fenton and Max located the red door Mr. Binks had told them about. Fenton opened it, and they found themselves in another room with a sloping attic ceiling. The room was freshly painted, and where the ceiling met a short wall, a gleaming row of computers sat on a long table. A man and a woman in gray coveralls were arranging some cables under the computers. Standing near them, with a confused look on her face, was a white-haired woman in a blue dress. Fenton recognized her as the museum librarian, Clara Ward.

"Now, tell me," she said, squinting at one of the computers, "if they're all connected, does that mean I have to have them all on at the same time?"

"Not at all, Miss Ward," said the man politely. "Each one can talk to the main computer downstairs, whether the others are on or not."

"Or they can talk to any of the other computers in the museum that are connected to the system," added the woman.

"Oh, my," said Clara, who hadn't seemed to notice that Fenton and Max had come into the room. "It's all so confusing.

And you say you're putting that computerized lock on the door, too. Here I am, the librarian, and I won't even be able to get in."

"It won't be that hard to learn, Miss Ward," said the woman, walking over to the door. "I'll put in a code that's easy for you to remember. When's your birthday?"

"October twelfth," she answered. Turning toward the entrance, she seemed to notice Fenton and Max for the first time. "Oh hello, boys. I'll be with you in a moment."

Fenton nodded, and Max went to take a seat at one of the computers.

"You see," said the woman in coveralls, "I've typed in your birthday, ten twelve, with this keypad. There'll be a keypad just like it outside this door. Now, if you want to de-activate the alarm and unlock the door, all you do is punch one zero one two."

"It even rhymes," said the other technician with a grin. "All you *do* is punch one zero one *two.*"

"Oh, yes, I suppose," said Clara Ward, looking a bit concerned. "But what would keep someone from just standing out there all night and trying every number until they got to my birthday?"

"Watch what happens when I try that," said the technician. She typed in a series of codes. "You have only four guesses. If you get it wrong on the fourth try, this is what happens."

A loud alarm filled the room. The technician pushed a couple of buttons, and the sound stopped.

"Oh my goodness," said Clara. "Well, I guess that solves that problem." She turned to Fenton and Max. "Now, what can I do for you young men? You know this area of the museum isn't open to the public just yet." She peered at Fenton more closely. "Why, it's Fenton Rumplemayer! I thought you were out west somewhere. How are your parents?"

"Fine, Miss Ward," said Fenton. "My dad and I are visiting here for Christmas. That's my friend Max. I hope it's okay for him to use that computer. He's kind of a computer genius."

"Oh, quite all right," said Clara. "That's what they're here for, isn't it? Besides, I could use a computer genius around here. Is that what you've come for, to see the new computer center?"

"Actually, I've also got a history report to do," said Fenton. "I want to write it about the old days of the museum. You know, the first dinosaur exhibits and stuff like that."

"Oh, I think I may have a few things for you to look at in the library," said Clara, motioning toward a doorway at the end of the computer room. "Although I suppose *this* is part of the library too, now. Well, come with me into the old library, in the turret."

She led the way through a door. Inside, Fenton found the original library just as he'd remembered it. There was a large circular area in the middle filled with wooden tables and chairs. Around this center area, arranged like pieces of pie, were alcoves with bookshelves. Some of the alcoves had tables in the middle, and others were closed off by folding wooden doors. The library was in one of the four round turrets that marked the corners of the museum, and the wall around its edge was gently rounded, with skinny little windows in the back of each alcove.

The librarian headed over to a small, old-fashioned fireplace between two of the alcoves. Inside it was a birch-log candle holder with four red candles.

"I'm just going to light my little Christmas display over here now that I have a visitor," she said, stooping down to light the candles. "It's so much nicer with real candles, I think." She returned the matches to the mantel above the fireplace.

Clara opened the folding doors to one of the alcoves. There was a gently curved bookshelf at the back and wood paneling trimmed with a pattern of intertwining vines on the side wall. The shelves inside were lined with boxes, books, and even some small models and fossils. A wooden table stood in the center of the room, and Fenton noticed a large wooden cabinet to one side.

"This area's used as a bit of a storage space," explained Miss Ward. She sighed. "It's supposed to be for historical materials, and there are some in the cabinet over there, but someone got the idea that this alcove was a good place to stick all the stuff the museum has no real use for anymore. It's all been a mess forever. I guess I'll try to fix it up a little in the new year. After all, now that we're getting that fancy new computer center, the rest of the library had better look its best too."

Fenton gazed around him. The place certainly did seem disorganized. A small model of a canoe sat on a shelf next to a glass case of mounted butterflies. There were several stacks of dusty books, and a cardboard box labeled 100TH ANNIVERSARY COMMEMORATIVE PINS was precariously balanced on one of them.

Clara searched for a moment through the books that lined a few of the shelves and removed a slim volume.

"Try this," she said, handing it to Fenton. "I'll be in the front trying to understand those computers. Just let me know if you need anything else."

"Okay, thanks, Miss Ward," said Fenton, sitting down on the floor with his book.

He looked at the book. It was called *Early American Museums*, and it had a short chapter on the New York Museum of Natural History. He began to read.

The museum, Fenton learned, was first opened in the 1800s by the Van Rensselaers, one of New York's rich old families. It was originally called the Van Rensselaer Museum of Pre-Historic Life, and was very popular. As Fenton turned the pages he found some drawings of the museum's early exhibits, many of which were pretty inaccurate. In one picture there were animals that were supposed to be dinosaurs but were shaped more like bears. Another showed a sculpted iguanodon that had been copied from one in England that had a spiked nose! Fenton knew that this was because when fossils of iguanodon were first discovered, only one of its thumb spikes was found, and the spike had been assumed to be a nose horn.

As Fenton read the descriptions of the early discoveries displayed in the museum, he thought about how hard it must have been for early paleontologists and reconstruction artists to try to create full skeletons from the few bones that had been found. According to the book, scientists often had to just guess at what part of a dinosaur the bones came from. Sometimes they even had to make up bones that were missing.

Fenton turned another page and read that the Van Rensselaers had lost all their money in a crash of the stock market. The Museum of Pre-Historic Life had closed its doors and gone out of business.

Several years later, a group of New Yorkers who were interested in paleontology and what they called Natural History had opened another museum in the original Van Rensselaer building. They called the new museum the New York Museum of Natural History.

Then Fenton came to a passage that read:

> The reputation of the New York Natural History Museum suffered a major blow upon the discovery of the Hoax of the Raptor's Claw—sometimes referred to as the Binks Affair—which shook the young museum to its very roots and almost cost it the confidence of the public.

What was the "Hoax of the Raptor's Claw"? Fenton wondered. He continued reading, but the passage didn't describe it any further. He read the paragraph again. Whatever the hoax was, it had also been known as the "Binks Affair." Could it have something to do with the Mr. Binks he and Max had met in the attic?

Fenton had read about scientific hoaxes before. There was Piltdown Man, for example. It was supposed to be the skull of a caveman, but was actually made from the skull of a human and the jaw of an orangutan. It had confused scientists for years until it was finally exposed as a fraud.

Could Mr. Binks really have been mixed up in something like that? Fenton wondered.

"Fenton?" said a voice.

Fenton looked up and saw Max, who was coming into the turret with Clara Ward behind him.

"Oh, hi," said Fenton.

"This friend Max of yours is marvelous!" said Miss Ward, her eyes bright with excitement. "He showed me everything about the computers. And he made it all so easy to understand!"

"I'd hardly call it everything," said Max. He looked a little embarrassed. "But we went through a bunch of stuff. That's a great system you have there, Miss Ward. And you're hooked up to the Internet, too."

"Really?" said Fenton eagerly. He had recently learned about the Internet, which was an information network that connected computers all over the world and which allowed people to communicate by e-mail. "Can we use it?"

"I'll show you how another time," said Max. "I have to go home for Hanukkah now. But we can do it on my computer, or even on your dad's laptop."

"I don't think my dad's connected to the Internet," said Fenton.

"No problem," said Max. "If that computer has a modem and I've got a disk and my father's password, then it's on the Internet." Max's father worked with computers.

"I guess I'll head out with you and look for my dad," said Fenton. "He told me they gave him an office to use on the third floor. I hope I can find it without running into Mr. Smythe."

Miss Ward sighed. "Has he been bothering you about the rules?"

Fenton nodded.

"He's that way with everyone," she said. "It's important to have rules, of course, but the way he enforces them! He's been here only four months, and he's already managed to upset just about everyone."

"I can see why," said Fenton. "Anyway, thanks for finding that book for me, Miss Ward. I know you don't lend books out, but is it okay if I come back to look for more things for my report?"

"Certainly. You're quite welcome," she answered. "And you can bring your friend Max with you anytime, too. I still have a lot more to learn!"

Fenton and Max went through the computer area and stopped in front of the red door, peering into the hall to look for Mr. Smythe. There was no sign of him, so they walked along the corridor and started down the grand stairway.

"Uh-oh," said Max, when they'd reached the landing halfway down to the third floor, "I think I see a bald head coming up the stairs."

Fenton looked around and spotted an open gallery across the landing.

"Come on," he said. "Let's make a run for that gallery. If we make it, he won't be able to say we're in an unauthorized area."

They tore down the stairs and raced through the gallery doorway, just as Mr. Smythe's head came bobbing over the edge of the staircase. Fenton jammed his hands in his pockets and leaned casually against a wall, and Max pretended to be intently studying a glass case filled with stuffed penguins.

Mr. Smythe glared at them both before continuing up the stairs. After he'd rounded the landing, the two boys burst into laughter.

"Okay," said Fenton, taking a deep breath. "I guess now I have to dive back into the danger zone to find my father's office."

"You've probably got a few minutes," said Max, grinning. "He must have gone up there to do something."

"Okay, see you later," said Fenton.

A few minutes later Fenton made his way down a corridor lined with dark, polished wood doors with little brass number plates on them and large, old-fashioned doorknobs. He found his father's office at the end of the corridor. It had the same doorknob and number plate as the others, but in addition, there was a brass plaque on it. It read:

> *This office was once occupied by Andrew Van Rensselaer,*
> *founder of the first museum on this site, the Van Rensselaer*
> *Museum of Pre-Historic Life. Following the opening of the*
> *New York Museum of Natural History in the buildings built*
> *by Andrew Van Rensselaer, his son, Tipton Van Rensselaer,*
> *occupied this office as well.*
>
> —*Metropolitan Historical Society*

Wow, thought Fenton. His father was using the same office that the founder of the original museum and his son had used. He wondered if that would be something good to put in his history report.

He tapped lightly on the door and turned the handle. Inside, he found his father sitting at an antique wooden desk in a large, wood-paneled room. One wall of the room was curved and had a tall, narrow window in it. His father was studying some papers and didn't seem to notice that Fenton had come in.

"Hi, Dad," said Fenton.

"Oh, hello, son," said his father, looking up. "I see you managed to find me. Nice office, isn't it?"

"It's definitely a lot bigger than the one you and Mom had," agreed Fenton.

The Rumplemayers' old office in the museum had been crowded, its two desks covered with books, papers, and even bones. Thinking of it reminded Fenton of Mr. Binks' cubbyhole in the attic. It was smaller and more cluttered than any place Fenton had ever seen.

"Hey, Dad," said Fenton, "what was the Binks Affair? Did it have anything to do with Mr. Binks who does the reconstructions?"

Mr. Rumplemayer leaned back from his desk. "So you've met Mr. Binks, have you?" he said in surprise. "I thought he never talked about the Binks Affair."

"He didn't," said Fenton. "I saw something about it in this book I was reading for my history report. The Hoax of the Raptor's Claw, they called it. Was there really a hoax?"

"I'm afraid there was, son," said Mr. Rumplemayer. "It was way before your mother's and my time here, back when Mr. Binks was a very young man. One of the rising stars on the museum staff, they said."

"What happened?" asked Fenton.

"Well, supposedly Mr. Binks assembled some bones and claws that he claimed were the hand of an oviraptor," explained Mr. Rumplemayer. "One of the first oviraptors discovered in Mongolia by a team from the museum."

"Wow," said Fenton, imagining what it must have been like to see some of the first known fossils of an oviraptor, a six-foot-long, crested dinosaur with large-clawed hands.

"It was very exciting news," agreed Fenton's father. "The newspapers called it the Raptor's Claw and made a big fuss over it. There were impossible problems shipping fossils back in those days. Many of them were lost or damaged, and I can see how things might have become confused. But still, that was no excuse for what happened. The oviraptor's hand was shown to be an outright fraud."

"You mean it was a fake?" said Fenton, amazed.

"That's right, son," said his father, shaking his head.

"Wow," said Fenton. He was kind of surprised to hear that a master craftsman like Mr. Binks, with all his skill and patience, would use his talent to create a hoax. It seemed a little strange.

Just then there was a rap on the office door, and a young man Fenton recognized as Greg Boyle, one of the assistants in the pale-ontology department, stuck his head in.

"Hey!" said Greg with a smile. "Fenton, hi. How are you doing?"

"Hi, Greg," said Fenton.

"Mr. R, a fax just came in for you down the hall," said Greg. He put a piece of paper on Fenton's father's desk. "Catch you later, Fenton."

"Okay, bye, Greg," said Fenton as the assistant closed the door behind him.

"This may be some good news, Fenton," said Mr. Rumple-mayer with a smile. He picked up the fax and read it. His face brightened even more, and he handed it to Fenton.

Fenton took the piece of paper.

34

It read:

Dear Bill—

Wonderful news—I've been able to arrange a flight to New York! I arrive Friday at 2:00 P.M. Please tell Fenton I can't wait to see him! It seems it's going to be a very merry Christmas for us all.

Love, Anne

"Mom's coming for Christmas?" said Fenton incredulously. He hadn't seen his mother since the summer, when she'd left for India and he and his father had moved to Wyoming.

His father smiled a huge smile. "That's what it says, son."

"This is great!" said Fenton. Now it could be like a real Christmas after all, with the whole family there, and his mother's good cooking, too. Maybe they'd could even get a tree! His mother was coming on Friday, which meant he'd see her in just three days.

"It certainly is," agreed his father. "To tell you the truth, I was afraid we were going to have a slightly lonely Christmas together."

"And now Mom will be here for the opening of the new Mesozoic Hall, too," said Fenton.

"Yes, I'm sure she'll be very interested in taking a look at some of those new reconstructions," said his father.

At the mention of reconstructions, Fenton thought again of old Mr. Binks in the attic. He pictured the tiny, crowded cubbyhole with its fossil pieces and carefully mounted tools. It certainly did seem strange that someone who seemed to care so much about his work would have been involved in a hoax.

4

"'Sam,'" Fenton read aloud from the computer screen. "Who's that?" It was Friday afternoon. Fenton and Max were sitting in front of Mr. Rumplemayer's laptop computer in the Palmers' living room, and Max was showing Fenton how to use the Internet. He had already demonstrated several steps to connect the laptop with a much larger computer by modem.

"SAM stands for Simple Access Method," said Max. "With SAM we can pick a subject and then look around the world for a computer that has something about that subject in it."

Fenton glanced toward the living-room windows, which faced the street. He was trying to concentrate on what Max was showing him, but it was hard. His father was due back from the airport with his mother any minute. Fenton and his father had bought a Christmas tree and some logs for the fireplace the night before. They didn't have any ornaments to put on the tree, though, so it stood in the living room next to the logs, looking bare. It still didn't feel much like Christmas.

Fenton turned back to the computer. The best way to make the time go by was probably to concentrate on what Max was showing him. Besides, he'd wanted to find out more about the Internet since it had helped his father's team win the McAlpin competition.

"Okay, pick a topic," said Max, pointing to the little blinking cursor on the screen next to the word **subject**.

Fenton didn't have to think very hard. "Dinosaurs."

DINOSAUR, Max typed.

"Here we go," he said. "We're getting on the information superhighway. That's what they call the thousands of computers linked together in the Internet and other computer networks."

"I get it," said Fenton.

"It's great," said Max. "You can send someone a message over it—that's e-mail—or you can go and look stuff up in other computers." He pointed to a list of abbreviations on the screen. "These are code names for different computers. SAM knows we're interested in dinosaurs, so it's only showing us computers with stuff about dinosaurs in them. As soon as we pick one of them, SAM'll get us into their computerized dinosaur files."

"Wow, really?" said Fenton.

"Sure," said Max. He used the mouse to choose one of the computers from the list. "Okay, now we're in a computer in California. Look at all this."

Fenton could hardly believe his eyes. On the screen in front of him was a list of dozens of dinosaur topics.

"Those are electronic file names," Max explained. "And that's only one page. Check out what it says in the corner there—'first of sixteen pages.'" He scrolled down. "What should we look at?"

"How about this one?" suggested Fenton, pointing to **dinosaur eggs: cat-scanning**.

Max hit a few keys. The list disappeared and was replaced by the words:

CAT-SCANNING DINOSAUR EGGS
BY EDGAR WUMDINK
SCIENCE AND TECHNOLOGY MAGAZINE
PRESS ENTER FOR ABSTRACT

"I guess that's a magazine article," said Max.

"Can we see it?" asked Fenton.

"Not the article itself," said Max. "But we can read all about it. That's what the abstract is. Here, all you have to do is press enter."

Fenton reached over and hit the key. He began to read.

> Cat-scanning, a method of obtaining detailed images of the human brain, has been used recently to explore inside dinosaur eggs without disturbing the delicate fossils.

"This is great," said Fenton as he skimmed the rest of it. "It's almost like reading the article itself."

"There are tons of these to look at," said Max. "And now that you can log on, you can use the Internet whenever you want."

Just then there was a noise at the front door. Fenton jumped up from his seat.

"Mom!" he yelled, dashing out to the entry area.

There, walking in the door, was his mother. She put her bags down and stretched out her arms.

"Hello, sweetheart!" she said as he reached her. "I've missed you so much." They gave each other a huge hug.

"I missed you, too, Mom," said Fenton.

His mother looked from Fenton to his father and smiled, her

eyes shining. "Being with you two is the best Christmas present I could hope for." Mr. Rumplemayer helped her off with her coat, and she shivered a little. "I've been so cold since I got off the plane. I didn't have any real winter clothes over there."

"Well, I got your winter things out of storage for you," said Mr. Rumplemayer, hanging up the coats. "They're upstairs. But meanwhile, why don't we start a fire with that wood we got last night, Fenton?" They walked into the living room.

"A fireplace, how nice," said Fenton's mother. "Oh, hi Max."

Max got up and waved. "Hi, Mrs. Rumplemayer. Welcome back to New York."

"Thank you. I'll just get myself a cup of tea," she said, heading for the kitchen.

"Why don't you bring that newspaper over and those logs, boys, so we can start the fire," said Mr. Rumplemayer.

"There's some cocoa in here for hot chocolate," called Mrs. Rumplemayer from the kitchen. "I'll have it ready in a minute."

"Oh, and wait till you see what your mother had me pick up on our way home," said Mr. Rumplemayer. He reached into a paper bag. "Christmas tree lights!"

A little while later the fire was roaring and the lights were on the tree. Fenton's mother had turned on the Palmers' stereo, and Christmas carols were playing.

Max sat at the computer, sipping his hot chocolate. Fenton took a spot on the carpet in front of the fire. Mr. Rumplemayer sank into the couch and took his shoes off.

Mrs. Rumplemayer joined him there and rested her head on his shoulder. She yawned and smiled at the same time.

"Sorry," she said, "it's two o'clock in the morning for me. I mean, that's what time it is in India. There's so much I want to ask about, but I'm too sleepy." Her eyes were half closed, but she kept smiling.

"And you have to tell us about India too, Mom!" said Fenton.

"Hmmm, yes, sweetheart," she said. "And we can string some popcorn for the tree tomorrow too." Her voice was drifting. Fenton could tell she was falling asleep.

Later that night Fenton lay awake in his third-floor bedroom, unable to sleep. He seemed to be thinking about everything at once—his mother, Mr. Binks and the hoax, the Internet, even his history report.

He looked out the window. It had started to snow lightly, and the snowflakes drifted lazily down into the yards below. Beyond the row houses he could see the top of the museum's wall, illuminated by street lamps, and the slate roof above it. In the little window in the museum's attic, the single light glowed. It was probably Mr. Binks's office, Fenton realized.

Fenton pictured Mr. Binks, sitting up in the museum's attic with his fossils and his tools. Now Fenton understood why the old man was hidden away up there. And why he looked so sad. He must have felt horrible after the hoax was discovered. And it probably ruined his reputation. The museum probably didn't want people to see him and be reminded of the hoax, either.

Fenton turned over in bed and tried to sleep, but he couldn't seem to stop thinking about Mr. Binks. Something about the story of the hoax just didn't make sense. Could a man who was

capable of putting together a beautiful specimen like that comp-sognathus Fenton had seen in his office actually be guilty of creating a fake oviraptor's hand? The more Fenton thought about it, the less he believed it was true.

But what other explanation could there be? If only he had more information on the hoax.

Suddenly, Fenton remembered the Internet. He was pretty sure he remembered how to log on from his father's lap top. Maybe there'd be some information about the Hoax of the Raptor's Claw—if it really *had* been a hoax—somewhere on the Internet.

He decided to find out. He pulled his heavy sweater over his pajamas and tiptoed down the stairs.

The Christmas tree lights filled the first floor with colors, reflecting off the shiny wood floor. Fenton went over to the other end of the room and sat down at the computer. He switched it on, and its screen gave off a blue glow.

He followed the steps Max had shown him to log on to the Internet and to access SAM. The cursor blinked next to the word subject. Fenton wondered what word he should type in.

"Scandal"? No, that would give all sorts of answers; there must have been hundreds of scandals. "Hoax"? Same problem. He decided to try hoax of the raptor's claw.

Nothing happened.

At first he thought he'd made a mistake, but then he realized it probably meant the SAM program couldn't find any computers with files on that exact topic. But there still could be some information on it in other files.

He thought again. Then he typed **new york museum of natural history**. Almost at once a list of ten computers appeared.

"All *right*," he whispered, choosing a computer.

The screen filled with listings almost at once. And the note in the corner said there were twelve pages to look at.

Fenton scrolled down the list.

ALBATROSS
ANT COLONIES
ARTS AND CRAFTS—PUBLICATIONS

On the eighth page he came to a title that looked good.

NY NTRL HIST MUSEUM—EARLY HISTORY

He selected it as Max had, and hit *enter* for the abstract. It was long. Good, he thought. Maybe this has something in it about the scandal.

On the screen was a brief description of the Van Rensselaer Museum of Pre-Historic Life and how it had failed. Since he had already read about that in the library, Fenton skipped ahead.

After describing the reopening of the museum and the expeditions it sent to Mongolia, the text said:

> A rivalry developed between Tipton Van Rensselaer, son of the old museum's founder, and a young man named John Binks. Binks came from humble origins and had no formal training in paleontology, but he still managed to outshine all the other reconstruction specialists then working in America.

Wow, thought Fenton. Mr. Binks had taught himself all about

43

dinosaurs. He continued reading.

> Binks's dedication to his work and careful attention to detail earned him the respect and admiration of the scientific community. His first reconstruction for the museum, an apatosaurus (at the time called "brontosaurus" by the paleontological community), was one of the earliest attempts to display a fossilized skeleton in a lifelike pose. It graces the museum's entrance hall to this day.

Fenton knew the apatosaurus skeleton well. He had sketched it many times, and had always liked the way it had been posed, with its head down, as if it were foraging for food. He supposed it must have been pretty difficult to set the bones in that position.

The description continued:

> Mr. Binks's reputation and career suffered later when he was accused of creating a fraudulent oviraptor's arm. The Hoax of the Raptor's Claw, as it was called, caused quite a stir. It was investigated by the Smythe Commission, headed by City Attorney Edmund Smythe.

Smythe! Fenton thought. He wondered if this Smythe was any relation to the Mr. Smythe who had been causing him so much trouble at the museum. He continued reading.

> The scientists on the commission examined all the evidence. Their verdict: Mr. Binks's oviraptor arm had been a poor attempt to fool the scientific community and the patrons of the New York Museum of Natural History.

5

The sun streamed in through the kitchen window and caught Mrs. Rumplemayer's hair as she threw back her head in laughter.

"And that monkey would not leave me alone," she said, catching her breath. "It climbed all over the dig site after me, absolutely insisting that I give it my food, which I wouldn't do."

Fenton and his father laughed too.

"Maybe it was hungry, Mom," said Fenton.

"Well, son, feeding an animal in the wild can make it forget how to find food on its own," said Fenton's father.

"That's right," said Fenton's mother. She laughed again. "Besides, *I* was hungry, and that curry had been specially made for me in the village."

It was Saturday, and Fenton had been listening all morning to his mother's stories about India. From what he had heard, India sounded like an amazing place. His mother had described cows that walked in the streets, and trains that were so crowded that people climbed up onto the roofs to ride them. She had told them about beautiful old carved stone temples, and colorful open-air markets that sold everything from fruit to sandals to gold-threaded silks. It all sounded so different from anything Fenton had ever seen.

"Oh, look how the time has flown," said his mother, looking at her watch. "Fenton, you should leave now if you want to meet Maggie's train."

"Oh, right, Mom," said Fenton, jumping off his stool.

"And I'd better head over to the museum," said his father.

"I'll probably bring Maggie over there later," said Fenton. "I've told her so much about it, I'm sure she'll want to see it."

Mrs. Rumplemayer stretched her arms above her head.

"How glorious it is not to have anything to do at all," she said. "I've been working so hard these last months. I think I'll have a long bath and read the paper. And then maybe I'll make a batch of Christmas cookies to put on the tree."

"Mmm," said Fenton. He loved his mother's homemade cookies. "Make gingerbread, okay, Mom?"

"Gingerbread it is," Mrs. Rumplemayer answered. She smiled. "And I guess I'll have to make a few extras to leave *off* the tree, too."

A little while later, Fenton stood at the station gate where Maggie's train was arriving. People were streaming out of it.

He almost didn't recognize Maggie at first. She was wearing shiny black shoes and a fancy-looking gray wool coat with a black velvet collar. Looking down at her legs, Fenton realized that she must be wearing a dress under the coat. Fenton stared in amazement. In all the months he'd known Maggie, he'd never once seen her in anything but jeans.

"Maggie, over here!" he called, making his way through the crowd of people toward her.

She saw him and smiled.

"Hi, Fen," she said, when they reached each other. She made a face and rolled her eyes. "My aunt Margaret thinks you have to get dressed up when you go to 'the City,' as she calls it. Believe me, it wasn't my idea."

"Don't worry about that," said Fenton. "Here you'll fit in no matter how you look."

But Maggie didn't look convinced.

"Where are we going?" she asked.

"You want to walk over to Rockefeller Center?" suggested Fenton. "They have a huge Christmas tree there."

"Oh, I saw that on TV," said Maggie. "Sure. But don't forget that I have to do some Christmas shopping while I'm here. And I definitely want to go to the museum, too."

"We can go up there from Rockefeller Center," said Fenton as they stepped outside. "Then you can do your shopping on the way."

"Wow," said Maggie, looking up at the buildings as they started to walk. "This is like being at the bottom of the Grand Canyon or something."

Fenton laughed. "Stop staring up in the air, or you'll look like a dumb tourist!"

"I *am* a tourist," she said, grinning. "Besides, don't forget, you looked kind of lost when you first got to Morgan Elementary, Fen."

They walked on, and a short while later they arrived at Rockefeller Center, a group of tall buildings lining a plaza full of Christmas displays and a skating rink. They looked at the huge tree, listened to some carolers, and watched the ice skaters for a few minutes. Then they bought some roasted chestnuts and headed in the direction of the museum and the Palmers' brownstone.

"I wonder how Willy's doing in Hawaii?" said Fenton as he broke open a hot chestnut with his cold fingers.

"It must be weird to be swimming at Christmas time," said Maggie. She looked over at a little antique shop. "Hey, let's go in there. Maybe I can find something for Aunt Margaret. She loves old things."

They walked over to the store. A little brass bell on the door jingled as they opened it.

The shop was crowded with used furniture, fancy old lamps, and glass cases filled with everything from antique toys to jewelry. On one of the cases an orange striped cat was stretched out. Stroking it was a thin young man in a sweater decorated with reindeer.

"Hi, kids," he said. "Welcome to the Home of the Unusual. If you can't find it someplace else, we probably have it here. What can I help you with?"

"I have to get something for my great-aunt," said Maggie, peering into one of the cases.

"Great-aunt, great-aunt," muttered the man, moving behind the counter. "What about a brooch?" he said, reaching into one of the shelves and taking out a tray of old jewelry. "Great-aunts are usually quite fond of brooches."

"Those are really nice, but Aunt Margaret already has lots of brooches and pins," said Maggie. "In fact, she has so many that they don't even fit in her jewelry box."

The man looked a little disappointed, but then his face brightened. "I may have just the thing for Great-Aunt Margaret," he said, reaching up to a shelf behind the counter.

He took down a small wooden box with an old-fashioned key sticking out of a keyhole at the front. The sides and top of the box were made of little wood panels with raised pieces of trim between them. He opened it, and they could see that the inside was lined with dark purple cloth.

"Just the thing for those extra brooches and pins," said the man. "And here's the best part." He turned the box around. "It has a secret catch in the back, which"—he felt around under the box—"opens this panel."

The panel snapped open with a pop.

"There we are," he said. "Your aunt can keep something very special in there and no one will ever know."

Maggie picked up the price tag that was attached to the key and looked at it.

"I don't know if I have that much with me," she said doubtfully.

"I can give it to you for thirty percent off," said the man. "That price is just for the tourists."

Maggie grinned at Fenton.

"Then I'll take it," she said.

A little while later, they arrived at the museum. Inside, Fenton decided to take a chance on running into Mr. Smythe and show Maggie the new Mesozoic Hall.

Stepping through the door in the plywood wall, he saw that the huge diplodocus skeleton had been completed and that several other displays were being set up or wheeled into place. In addition, a few people were putting up Christmas and Hanukkah decorations, and others were setting up tables.

"It looks like they're getting ready for a party in here," said Maggie.

"Oh, I almost forgot about the big holiday party," said Fenton. "It's tonight."

Just then he caught sight of Mr. Binks walking in their direction. And with him was with Mr. Smythe! Quickly Fenton motioned to Maggie to join him behind a skeleton of a young spinosaurus, hoping that the bony "swords" jutting up from the dinosaur's backbone would shield them from Mr. Smythe's view.

"That tall bald guy likes to throw kids out of here," Fenton explained to Maggie.

They could hear Mr. Smythe talking on the other side of the spinosaurus. He sounded angry.

"Listen here, Binks," he said. "Finish putting that pterodactyl up now or I'm going to see Director Soames about your stubbornness. This is the most important night of the year, and it better not be ruined because of some mistake you imagine's been made in a pterodactyl's neck bone."

"It's a pteranodon, and I'm not going to put its head on until we've corrected the vertebrae," said Mr. Binks. "If we don't have time to do it before the party, we can just leave it out of the display."

"No one's going to notice a couple of out-of-place vertebrae, Binks," said Mr. Smythe. "Besides, if they do, we can always cover it up somehow."

50

"Well, I'm not going to do it. It's not right," said the old man. "I'll just try to get the vertebrae fixed in time for the opening."

"I've had just about enough of your lack of cooperation, Binks," snarled Mr. Smythe. Fenton could see the back of his head between two of the spinosaurus' "swords," and it was turning bright red. "When the director gets here, she's going to hear about this!" He stomped off in a huff, and Mr. Binks made his way to the back of the exhibit hall.

"That guy Smythe sure is mean," said Maggie. "I mean, he was really nasty to that old man."

"Yeah," agreed Fenton. "That's Mr. Binks he was yelling at."

"I don't see why he had to act that way," said Maggie. "After all, Mr. Binks was just trying to get it right."

"I know," said Fenton. "That's what makes this whole thing so hard to understand."

"What's that?" asked Maggie.

"Years ago, Mr. Binks was accused of creating a hoax," Fenton explained. "It was the arm of an oviraptor he had put together."

"Oviraptor," said Maggie. "Doesn't that mean 'egg-thief'?"

"That's right," said Fenton. "They found the first one on a pile of what they thought were protoceratops eggs, so they decided it was stealing them. Actually, though, it turned out that the eggs were oviraptor eggs, and that the dinosaur was just taking care of its babies."

"Wow, I guess oviraptor had a pretty bad reputation for a while," said Maggie, laughing a little. "So, what about this hoax?"

"Well, apparently the arm turned out to be a fake," said Fenton. "It was a big scandal for the museum. The newspapers called it the Hoax of the Raptor's Claw."

"That's weird. That old man just doesn't seem like a cheat to me," said Maggie firmly. "Do they know for sure it was him?"

"It sounds like it, but I don't know," said Fenton. He saw Mr. Binks heading back toward them with the vertebra in his hand. "I first found out about the whole thing when I was looking up stuff for my history report in the museum library. But now I'm beginning to wonder if it really happened the way they say it did. I mean, maybe I can come up with something more in the library. Something that will show for sure whether Mr. Binks really did it."

"*Very* interesting," said a voice from behind them.

They whirled around. Standing there was Mr. Smythe, his beady eyes focused right on Fenton.

"Well, my fine young troublemaker," said Mr. Smythe, his face starting to turn red. "Once again I find you in an unauthorized area. And you have an accomplice this time!"

Fenton saw Maggie's eyes widen. What would Mr. Smythe do to them?

"I demand to see your supervising staff member," said Mr. Smythe. "If he or she is not in this immediate vicinity, you are going to be in trouble to the fullest extent permitted by law."

Fenton gulped. He was pretty sure Maggie's aunt Margaret wouldn't be too happy if she had to come to New York to get Maggie out of jail.

"These young people are under my supervision," said a voice next to them. Fenton turned his head. Standing nearby was Mr. Binks, his jaw raised slightly in the air.

53

"Mr. Binks, what do you suppose we are running here, an *elementary school?*" demanded Smythe.

"No," said Mr. Binks firmly, "a museum. And museums are for people, not rules. So I'll thank you to leave us in peace."

Smythe turned even redder, sputtered a bit without being able to speak, and once again marched off.

"Thanks a lot, Mr. Binks. You really saved us," said Fenton.

"Well, I know the difference between a youngster who's making trouble and one who's really interested in dinosaurs. Something Mr. Smythe will never understand," said Mr. Binks. "Now, if you'll excuse me, I've got these vertebrae fixed, and I want to get that pteranodon up."

He went off to where two workers were standing next to the headless pterosaur that had been lowered from the ceiling.

"I'm telling you," said Maggie, gazing after him, "that is *not* the kind of person who would be part of a hoax."

"So you see what I mean," said Fenton. "Come on, let's go to the library. Maybe we can dig up some more information."

On the fourth floor, to Fenton's surprise, they almost ran into Mr. Smythe again! He was hurrying out of the library, and they managed to hide by scooting around a corner.

"What is *he* doing here?" said Fenton in a whisper.

"It's almost like he raced up to get here before we did," said Maggie.

They waited until he had passed, and then went into the library, where they found Clara Ward typing on one of the computer keyboards. Fenton went over to her and waited until she looked up.

"Well, hello there, Fenton," she said cheerfully. "Look at me using this thing, as though I've been doing it my whole life. And I owe it all to your friend Max."

"That's great, Miss Ward," said Fenton. "This is my friend Maggie Carr from Wyoming."

"Hi," said Maggie.

"It's a pleasure to meet you," said Miss Ward.

"We were wondering if we could see some more stuff about the early days of the museum," said Fenton.

"Well, I must say, you certainly are interested in the old times around here," said Miss Ward. "Usually people want to look up things about dinosaurs in this library."

"It's just that I read about the Hoax of the Raptor's Claw the other day," said Fenton. "I'd like to find out some more about it."

At Fenton's words a shocked look came over the librarian's face, and for a few moments she was silent. Then she took a deep breath.

"The things you want will be in that alcove I showed you last time," she said without looking at them. "I don't know exactly where, possibly in the historic materials cabinet. As I said, the materials in there are a mess. They've never really been sorted out." She turned away.

"Wow, did you see how she changed when you mentioned the hoax?" whispered Maggie as she and Fenton headed toward the alcove.

"Yeah," said Fenton. "It seemed almost as though she was mad at us or something. I wonder why."

Fenton pulled open the folding doors to the alcove, and he

and Maggie stepped inside.

"Boy, this place *is* a mess," said Maggie, looking around. "It seems kind of strange. The rest of the library is so neat and organized." She peered into a cardboard carton on a shelf. "And what's all this stuff?"

"Miss Ward said she was going to clean it up after New Year's," Fenton told her. "The museum uses this area to store things. I think there are even some pieces from old exhibits."

Maggie pulled the carton off the shelf and set it on the floor.

"There sure is a lot of old junk in here," she said. She took something out of the box. "Hey, look at this. It's some kind of plaque, with a hadrosaur on it. But what's a hadrosaur doing in the water?"

"Let me see," said Fenton. Maggie handed him the plaque. Painted on it was a picture of a parasaurolophus, one of the hadrosaurids, or "duck-billed" dinosaurs. The parasaurolophus was shown neck deep in a lake, its feet paddling below the surface of the water. "People used to think that the hadrosaurs might have lived in the water," said Fenton. He pointed to the long crest on the dinosaur's head. "Some scientists even thought that this was a kind of a snorkel. Trouble was, there wasn't any opening in the end of it."

Maggie laughed. "Sounds like it would be pretty hard to breathe through a snorkel like that. I read somewhere that hadrosaurs used their head crests to make sounds."

"Yeah, that's what some people think," said Fenton. "But nobody's really sure. It could also have something to do with their sense of smell. It definitely wasn't a snorkel, though, since none of

56

the dinosaurs lived in the water."

"I guess that's why they took this down," said Maggie, taking the plaque from Fenton. She peered into the box again. "Boy, there sure is some funny old stuff in here."

As Maggie continued to look through the box, Fenton walked over to the historic-materials cabinet. Inside were stacks of paper and some books. A thin volume caught his eye. Its title was *New York Museum of Natural History—The Founding Years*. He pulled it out and sat down with it at the table in the center of the alcove. He flipped open the book to a page that showed an old black-and-white photograph of the museum and read the caption under the photo. It said:

> The first stage of the construction of what is now the New York Museum of Natural History was a corner turret and one wing. This part of the present museum was built by Andrew Van Rensselaer and operated as the Van Rensselaer Museum of Pre-Historic Life. Mr. Van Rensselaer did not live to see more of the museum constructed. After his death, the Natural History Museum Committee completed the other three corners of the museum and the central galleries.

Fenton thought a moment. If that brass plaque on his father's office was right and Andrew Van Rensselaer had worked downstairs, then he was sitting in the very turret that was in the photo. That meant the library turret and structure next to it were the original Museum of Pre-Historic Life. Fenton recognized the little guard booth in the photo as well. It must have been part of the Van Rensselaer Museum too.

Turning the page, Fenton found a floor plan of the original museum's first floor. But the corner of the page, where the turret would have appeared, had been cut off.

"Hey, what's this?" he said.

"What do you mean?" asked Maggie, standing up from her box and coming over.

Fenton turned the page again. To his amazement, the turret had been cut off of the second-floor plan also. There were two more floor plans, for the third and fourth stories, and sure enough, they both had the part with the turret cut off too!

"Look at this," he said. "These are floor plans of the museum, and there's this same piece missing from each page."

"Why do you think someone cut them all out like that?" said Maggie.

"I don't know," said Fenton, "but you know what's odd? It's this turret we're in now."

Just then Clara Ward hurried by the alcove, glancing quickly in at Fenton and Maggie as she passed.

"She's definitely acting funny," said Maggie.

"Yeah, I wonder why she got angry when we told her what we were looking for," said Fenton.

"Maybe she was upset, not angry," said Maggie. She stood up. "I'm going to talk to her and see what I can find out."

As Maggie walked back into the main library area, Fenton fingered the neatly sliced edges of the pages of the book. Who had cut off those corners? he wondered. And why?

He stood up from the table and gazed around the alcove for a moment. As he did, his eye was caught by the box that Maggie had been going through. He went over to it and bent down to look inside.

Maggie was right; the box was filled with an amazing assortment of old junk. There were bundles of old museum brochures, a few colorful pieces of rock mounted on a piece of polished wood, and a small stuffed bird of some kind that was missing one of its glass eyes. Then, near the bottom of the box, Fenton noticed a bundle about a foot long, wrapped in yellowed newspaper.

Curious, he lifted out the bundle. As he did, the newspaper cracked in his hands, and a few pieces of it flew in little bits down to the floor. It must be very old, Fenton realized.

Carefully, Fenton pulled at the layers of newspaper. Whatever was inside was long and narrow, and fairly light. He unwrapped the last of the paper and stared, dumbfounded, at what was in front of him. It was a dinosaur hand, an oviraptor's hand. And something definitely looked strange about it. Its three long fingers ended in sharp, slightly curved claws, but the joints of the fingers seemed oddly stuck together, and didn't flow evenly, as they should. In addition, the joints were fastened at the knuckles with thick wire, which had been pulled through several large, irregular holes in the bones. This was it, Fenton realized, the raptor's claw.

Fenton couldn't tell for sure from just looking at it if the hand was a fake or not. But there was one thing he thought he could be pretty certain of—that it didn't look like the work of Mr. Binks. It was almost impossible to imagine that the fastidious old man whose work Fenton had seen in the museum's attic, and whose delicate tools were so neatly arranged on his wall could have made this messy-looking reconstruction.

59

Just then Fenton heard a noise at the door to the alcove.

"Psst. Fen." It was Maggie. "I think I talked Miss Ward into telling us about the hoax," she said. "Come on, quick, before she changes her mind."

"Hang on," said Fenton. He held up the hand. "I found it. At least I think I have. This must be the oviraptor's hand that Binks was supposed to have made."

"You're kidding," said Maggie, hurrying over. She gazed down at the reconstruction. "So this is it, huh?"

"That's right," said Fenton. "And I'm almost positive that Mr. Binks isn't the one who made it. It just doesn't look like his work at all."

"Come on," said Maggie. "Let's go find out what Ms. Ward has to say about the whole thing. Maybe she can give us some more information."

Hurriedly, Fenton wrapped the hand in what was left of the newspaper and stuck it back into the box. He followed Maggie out to the main library area, where Clara Ward sat waiting for them.

Miss Ward's face had a grim expression.

"Sit down, children," she said. "I am not a gossip, but I do want to tell you about Mr. Binks."

Maggie and Fenton sat down. The library was still.

"Sometimes it's hard to talk about sad things that happened long ago," she said, "but I'm going to do my best."

"We appreciate it," said Maggie.

"Mr. Binks was a brilliant young paleontologist," Miss Ward began. "In those days it was an *art* to reconstruct dinosaur fossils, an art and a science. Of course, it is today, too, but then, because of difficult field conditions and the incomplete skeletons that were found, skillful reconstructions were based on intuition and a lot of good detective work. And Mr. Binks was a master."

"He still is," Fenton interrupted. "You should see the little compsognathus he put together. It's amazing!"

"Yes, I suppose he is," she said, seeming to lose her place in the story for a moment. "The main museum was still being built at the time I'm talking about, and what is now the library was a work and exhibit space. The alcoves were often used for small exhibits.

"Mr. Binks was working on reconstructing the oviraptor's arm in that very alcove where you've been sitting," Miss Ward went on, nodding toward the storage area. "He kept the folding doors locked. It was exacting work, and he wanted to do it in seclusion."

Fenton glanced at the heavy oak folding doors that separated the storage alcove from the center area.

"Dinosaur eggs and egg-stealing dinosaurs were big news that year," she went on. "The newspapers heard about Mr. Binks's project and made it into quite a story. You know, 'Dinosaur Scientist Builds Egg-Thief's Claw in Secret,' that sort of thing. They started calling it the Raptor's Claw, which, of course, made people even more interested. All this made Mr. Binks even more strict about the security in there. He opened the doors for no one. Finally, he announced that he would present the oviraptor's arm to the museum and the public."

"Wow," said Maggie. "That must have been pretty exciting."

"The presentation was quite an event," agreed Miss Ward.

"Much more than John, I mean Mr. Binks, imagined it would be. It was as though the Raptor's Claw had become a celebrity. There were cameras and a radio reporter covering the story live. Even my late husband, who was also a scientist, ran back to his office to get his journal at the last minute so he could take notes on the event. Anyway, I think Mr. Binks was taken aback by all the commotion. He's a bit shy, to tell the truth."

"Maybe that's why he didn't want to tell Max and me who he was," said Fenton, "when we first met him in his work room, I mean."

"He didn't?" said Miss Ward, a small smile coming to her lips. "Well, in any case, the crowd had assembled out here in the center, and Mr. Binks had set up the display so that the oviraptor arm was in a case in the middle of the alcove, right about where you've been working. At the appointed hour, he stepped out in front of the doors for his brief lecture, closing them behind him. When he was finished he opened up the doors, stepping aside. There was a big commotion, flashbulbs and a lot of pushing and shoving, and I believe Mr. Binks left."

"And that was it?" said Maggie.

Miss Ward looked sad.

"Until the rumors started," she said. "There were murmurs from several of the departing scientists, and the next day all the papers had the story, 'The Hoax of the Raptor's Claw.' There was quite a hullabaloo here at the museum, and finally the fossil was declared a fraud."

"But wait," said Fenton, thinking of the large wires and irregular holes he had seen in the reconstruction. "Maybe it wasn't Mr.

Binks's fault. Maybe he wasn't the one who made the fake arm, after all. Did anybody ever think of that?"

"Yeah," said Maggie. "Someone could have even switched Mr. Binks's arm with the fake."

Clara shook her head slowly. "Mr. Binks always claimed that the arm they examined wasn't the one that he had put together. And I very much wanted to believe him," she said softly. "Unfortunately, there was no possible way for the oviraptor arm to have been tampered with."

"But how do you know?" said Fenton. He was sure it couldn't be true.

"It would have been impossible," said Clara emphatically. "I know. I had just come back from Mongolia myself, and I was right here in front of those doors when it all happened."

6

An hour later, Maggie and Fenton entered the Palmers' brownstone. The smell of gingerbread cookies filled the air.

"Mom, we're home!" called Fenton as they took off their coats.

"Hi," called his mother from the kitchen. "You're just in time. Cookies will be ready in a moment."

Fenton led Maggie back to the kitchen.

"Hi, Mom," said Fenton. "This is Maggie."

"Well, hello, Maggie," said his mother, wiping her hands on a dish towel and coming over to shake hands with her. "It's nice to finally meet you."

"Don't worry, Mom," said Fenton. "Maggie doesn't usually look like this; her aunt Margaret made her dress up to come into the city."

"Well, I think you look delightful, Maggie," said his mother. "And those clothes will be just right if you want to come with us to the museum holiday party this evening."

"That's a great idea," said Fenton. He turned to Maggie. "All the exhibits will be up, and they usually have good stuff to eat."

"Sounds fun," said Maggie. "Except my aunt is expecting me home on the eight o'clock train."

"Well, that seems rushing things a bit," said Mrs. Rumplemayer. "After all, you just got here. Why don't I talk to Aunt Margaret and see if you can spend the night? You can have Jenny Palmer's bedroom on the second floor. It's quite charming."

"I'd love to stay, Mrs. Rumplemayer," said Maggie, "if Aunt Margaret says it's okay."

"Wonderful," said Fenton's mother. "But before we call her, how about some cookies and hot chocolate?" She opened the oven and took out a tray covered with steaming gingerbread cookies in the shapes of snowmen and Christmas trees. She began to lift them off the cookie tray and set them onto a big blue plate. "Now what have you two been up to today?"

"Actually, we've been trying to find out about something at the museum," said Fenton, sitting down at the counter across from his mother. "It's about Mr. Binks, and the Hoax of the Raptor's Claw. We're trying to figure out what really happened."

"That was an awfully long time ago," said his mother. "What makes you think there's something to solve?"

"Well for one thing, we found the fake oviraptor's arm," said Fenton.

"Really?" said his mother, raising her eyebrows. "You found the arm itself? I've never seen it."

"It's in this old box up in the library," said Maggie.

"And it looks like whoever made it did kind of a messy job," said Fenton. "That's one of the reasons I don't think it was Mr. Binks. I was up in his office, in the attic, and I saw some of his reconstructions. They're really great, not at all like the arm."

"But we had a talk with Miss Ward, the librarian," said Maggie, sitting down next to Fenton. "She said she was there when the hoax was discovered, and she can't see how he *couldn't* be guilty."

"Well, if anyone would have wanted to believe in him, it would have been Clara," said Mrs. Rumplemayer. "I guess she told you Mr. Binks had asked her to marry him at the time."

"Mr. Binks wanted to marry Miss Ward?" exclaimed Fenton.

"She didn't say a word about it!" said Maggie. "Are you sure?"

"Oh, quite sure, " said Mrs. Rumplemayer. "She hadn't said she would yet, though. She had another suitor at the same time, whom she did finally end up marrying."

"Boy, you sure know a lot about this, Mom," said Fenton.

Mrs. Rumplemayer poured three cups of hot chocolate.

"Yes, " she said, bringing them over to the counter, "I suppose you could say Clara Ward was my hero when I was a child."

"She was?" said Fenton. "Clara Ward the librarian?"

"Well now, librarians are fine people," said his mother, sitting down with them, "but this was way before she started working in the library. Clara was one of the first women in paleontology, though she was hardly more than a girl when she started out. She went on some of the early fossil-hunting expeditions to Mongolia."

"Really?" said Maggie, pulling her seat closer to Mrs. Rumplemayer.

"That's right," said Fenton's mother. "In those days a trip into Mongolia was an unbelievable adventure, full of hardships. Of course now we almost never remove fossils from the countries they're found in, but back then it was often done. As a child I used to read about Clara's exploits. She was one of the reasons I decided to study paleontology."

"Wow," said Fenton. "Who would have thought that old Miss Ward—"

"*I* would have," Maggie said firmly. "You can tell there's something strong underneath her soft appearance. But Mrs. Rumplemayer, why didn't she ever marry Mr. Binks, do you think? Was it because of the hoax?"

"Actually, in the end it was Mr. Binks who changed his mind about wanting to marry her," answered Fenton's mother. "After the arm was declared a fraud he turned into a bit of a hermit. The museum forced him up into that little office in the attic, and he just hid there. He wouldn't talk to anyone. Not even Clara."

"That's so sad," said Maggie, picking up a cookie.

"Yes," agreed Mrs. Rumplemayer. "A year later Clara married Tipton Van Rensselaer. He had asked her just about when Mr. Binks had, but people always said she never felt as strongly for him. Maybe that's one of the reasons she took back her own name, Ward, after he died. But in those days most women thought it was their duty to get married, and I think that had a lot to do with her decision."

"I read that Tipton Van Rensselaer and Mr. Binks were rivals in the museum, too," said Fenton. "They both wanted to become the director of exhibits."

"Oh really?" said his mother. "I wasn't aware of that." She picked up a cookie shaped like a snowman. "Anyway, Mr. Binks's behavior became very odd after the scandal. He seems to spend all of his time at work. Some people say he even sleeps up in his little room in the attic." She took a bite of the snowman.

Again, Fenton thought of the little light glowing late at night in the attic window of the museum.

"Well," said his mother with a sigh, "I think it's time we put a call in to Maggie's aunt Margaret. And then, if she says it's all right for you to stay, I think we should all start getting ready for the party."

Later that evening the Rumplemayers and Maggie, along with Max, whom they'd picked up on the way, walked into the museum. The holiday decorations were all up, and people milled about at the foot of the great marble stairs, which were closed off by red velvet ropes for the occasion.

"Hey, there's the mayor," said Fenton, who was dressed in a new white shirt his mother had brought him from India, and his dinosaur belt. "I recognize him from TV."

"And there's a TV camera crew in the new exhibit hall," said Max, craning his neck as they walked into the big gallery, which was full of people.

"I thought they'd never take down that wall with the 'Pardon Our Appearance' sign on it in time," said Mr. Rumplemayer.

"Or finish putting up the exhibit," said Maggie. "You should have seen this place this afternoon! And look at it now. I'm so glad Aunt Margaret said it was okay for me to stay."

"Just look at the posture of that diplodocus skeleton, how they have it protecting its youngster from that allosaur," said Mrs. Rumplemayer. "It's absolutely marvelous."

Just then, Jeff Masters, the paleontology student and guard who had saved Fenton from Mr. Smythe, walked over to them.

"Hello, everyone," he said. He glanced down at Fenton's belt. "Wow, Fenton, I hope you're careful about wearing that in the rain."

"Why?" asked Fenton.

"Well, you know, with something like that, you have to be real careful about tyranno-sau-*rust*." He grinned.

Fenton laughed and shook his head.

"Isn't the exhibit wonderful?" said Mrs. Rumplemayer. "And look at all there is to eat over there!"

The tables Fenton and Maggie had seen earlier were crowded with platters of food, and waiters were bringing even more through a door at the back of the exhibit hall.

"I had a bite earlier," said Jeff. "But I wish they were serving coffee. I go on duty soon."

"That's a shame, Jeff," said Mr. Rumplemayer. "Tonight of all nights."

"Well, I wanted to be able to have a few days off around Christmas to be with my family," Jeff explained. "So I offered to work tonight. Anyway, we'll have only a *skeleton* crew on." He grinned again as Fenton and his friends laughed. "Hey, it was nice seeing you all, but you'll have to excuse me. I've got to change into my uniform before eight."

"Oh, there's the director. Let's go say hello to her," said Fenton's mother to his father. "You kids will be all right by your-selves for a while, won't you?"

"Mom," said Fenton, rolling his eyes, "how many years have I been on my own at the holiday party?"

"Of course, Fenton," said his mother, "I keep forgetting how grown up you are." She took Mr. Rumplemayer's elbow. "We'll see you all later."

"Let's go get some food," said Maggie, eyeing the tables at the back of the room.

"Sounds good to me," said Fenton.

They made their way to the tables and loaded up their plates with turkey, stuffing, and pumpkin pie. Soon they were munching away.

"Look," said Maggie, "there's Miss Ward. Let's go talk to her."

Miss Ward was standing by herself, a punch glass in her hand. She was looking up at the pteranodon, its head now in place. She smiled when she saw them.

"Hello, Fenton. Hello, Maggie," she said. "Oh, and you've brought Max with you. How nice. The food's wonderful, isn't it?"

"It sure is," mumbled Max, his mouth full of pumpkin pie.

Maggie glanced up at the pteranodon. "Mr. Binks was working on that until almost the last moment this afternoon. I guess he figured out what was wrong with it. Do you think he'll come to the party, Miss Ward?"

"Oh no, Maggie, he never attends social occasions," said Miss Ward.

"Well, I guess sometimes a person just wants to be alone," said Maggie as the party buzzed around them.

"Yes," said Miss Ward, "people are like that, aren't they? My late husband, Tipton, was forever stealing off to his office to write about the museum in his journal. And who ever got to read it? No one, as far as I know, for all the time he spent on it." She stopped, watching something that was happening in another corner of the festivities. "My, my. Look at Mr. Smythe. I think he's actually pretending to be nice because it's Christmas."

Fenton thought of something. "Miss Ward, Mr. Smythe didn't have anything to do with the Smythe Commission, did he?"

"Oh, no, he's far too young," she answered. "But it was his grandfather, the city attorney, who headed the commission that investigated the hoax. He had a feud going with the first director of the museum, and I'm sure he enjoyed all the trouble he caused."

"Kind of like his grandson, *our* Mr. Smythe," said Fenton.

"It's a terrible thought," said Miss Ward, "but maybe being mean runs in the Smythe family. I'm going to go wish him a merry Christmas anyway. Even he deserves that at this time of year."

"I think I'd better just keep out of his way," said Fenton. "See you later, Miss Ward."

"Enjoy yourselves. Oh, and by the way, Max, I'll have a lot of questions to ask you about the computers next year," she said, her eyes twinkling.

"Next year?" said Max, looking confused.

"That's right," she answered. "The library's closed until January third, but right after New Year's I have a little project that I want to discuss with you. I just have to straighten out some details with the director."

Uh-oh, thought Fenton, the library's going to be closed till after New Year's. That was going to make it awfully hard for him to finish the investigation, not to mention his history report. He had to be back at school in Wyoming on January second.

"Anyway," said Miss Ward, "enjoy the party. And merry Christmas." She turned and walked off toward Mr. Smythe.

As soon as Miss Ward was gone, Maggie turned to Fenton and Max. "Did you hear what she said?"

"Yeah," said Fenton, dejected. "The library's going to be closed for over a week."

"Not that," said Maggie. "The other thing. The part about Tipton Van Rensselaer's journal. It could really be important, especially if he kept it as carefully as she says."

"That's a good point," said Max. "After all, Tipton was working at the museum then too. He probably wrote all about the scandal."

"In fact, didn't Miss Ward say that he went to get it so he could take notes on the exhibition of the arm?" said Maggie excitedly.

"You're right!" said Fenton. "If only we could find it." Then he had an idea. "What about the storage alcove up in the library? It's full of old stuff from the museum, and Miss Ward said it hadn't been cleaned out in years. After all, we found the oviraptor arm up there. Maybe there's a chance the journal could be there too."

"Maybe it's in that historic materials cabinet where you got that old book. Even if it isn't, there's bound to be more stuff in there somewhere about the scandal," said Maggie.

"But we can't get into the library," Fenton remembered. "It's closed."

"Hey," said Max, "what about that new electronic lock? Remember we were up there when they were setting it up?"

"That's right!" said Fenton. "Oh, but I'm not sure if I can remember the combination. Can you?"

"All I remember is they said you had four tries to get it right," said Max.

"Are you guys talking about what I think you're talking about?" asked Maggie with a grin.

"The way I see it, it's now or never," said Fenton firmly. "With someone going around cutting corners out of books, there's no telling how long that journal or anything else will stay in that alcove if there's anything important in it."

"But they have the stairs roped off," said Max. "We can't just go out there and climb over. Somebody's going to ask us where we're going."

"You're right," said Fenton, thinking for a moment. "I know! The service elevator, the one we passed in the hall near Mr. Binks's room, Max. It comes down here to the first floor, too. We'd have to go through about three galleries and a storage room to get there." He looked around. "I'm pretty sure that door back where the waiters are using would start us off in the right direction."

"But won't the lights be off in that part of the museum if they're not using it?" asked Max a little nervously.

"Probably most of them will," said Fenton. "But I think I'll be able to find it."

"Well, we really don't have any choice if we're going to get back into that alcove," said Maggie. "I say let's give it a try."

7

A few minutes later, Fenton, Maggie, and Max made their way through a deserted gallery filled with dinosaur skeletons. The pale blue night lights threw huge shadows around the big room. The noise from the celebration could barely be heard in the distance, and Maggie's boots clicked loudly on the polished stone floor.

"You know," said Max, "the farther we get from the party, the spookier this place is."

"I think it's cool," said Maggie. "It's like having the whole museum to ourselves."

Fenton agreed. He had always loved it when his parents worked late and he could be in the museum after hours, when all the visitors were gone. Still, this time he was a little nervous. He couldn't help wondering what would happen to them if they got caught. He had a feeling that, except for where the party was, the whole museum was an unauthorized area tonight.

They turned the corner into another gallery. A menacing spiked neck loomed out of the darkness in front of them.

"Yikes, what's that?" said Max, taking a step back.

"It's just the sauropelta," said Fenton as they walked past. "Those cones on its neck are part of its armor."

"This is so creepy," said Max, looking around.

"It's really just the shadows that are scaring us," said Maggie.

"*That's* not a shadow," whispered Max, stopping short. A pair of eyes glowed in the darkness.

Fenton took a quick breath. Was someone watching them? He tried to remember exactly where they were. Then he let out his breath in relief. "It's only the troodon restoration."

"*Only* a troodon," said Max.

Fenton took them into a store room. Parts of human figures were piled against the wall and hanging from the ceiling. Fenton heard Maggie catch her breath.

"Those are plaster cave-people parts. I think that means we're almost there." They rounded a dark corner. "Oh, good," said Fenton, relieved. "Here's the elevator."

They got into the old elevator and rode up to the fourth floor. The door opened, and they made their way quietly through the dimly lit hall to the red library door.

"Okay, you guys," said Maggie, "what's the code?"

Max shook his head. "I was too busy checking out all those new computers to really listen. But I do remember they were trying to make it easy for Miss Ward to memorize."

"I know," said Fenton. "They were using her birthday."

"Great," said Maggie. "When's her birthday?"

"I can't remember," Fenton admitted.

Maggie groaned.

"Maybe we should go back and ask her," suggested Max.

"Forget it," said Fenton. "We can't just walk up to her and ask her when her birthday is. It would seem too suspicious."

"Fen's right," said Maggie. "Besides, we're lucky we got up

here without anyone noticing us. We can't take the chance of sneaking down and back."

They were all silent for a moment.

"If we were in the library," said Max, "I could tap into the personnel files in the computer and look it up."

Fenton looked at him.

"Max, was that supposed to be a joke, or have you gone computer loony? If we were in the library, we wouldn't *need* to know her birthday." He thought a moment, trying to remember. "Now let's see, I think it was in the fall some time."

"Oh great, that cuts it down to ninety-two possible dates," said Max, looking up at the ceiling.

"Hold it, hold it, said Fenton, straining to remember again. "I'm pretty sure it started with a one."

"That still means it could be October, November, or December," said Maggie.

"Well, it wasn't December," said Fenton. "Someone would have said happy birthday. I think it was November tenth."

He typed 1-1-1-0 on the keypad. The red light kept blinking.

"Uh-oh," said Max.

"Hold on," said Fenton. "Maybe it was one one one nine."

He took a deep breath and punched in the numbers.

"If you don't get it on the fourth try, the alarms go crazy," said Max. "That part I remember very well."

"That means you have two guesses left, Fen," said Maggie.

Fenton swallowed.

"It was something like one zero two one, I'm sure of it," said Fenton. But he wasn't so sure at all. "Here goes." He tried 1-0-2-1.

"Wrong again," Max moaned.

Fenton's palms were sweating. Why couldn't he remember the right numbers?

"Fen," said Maggie. "There's only one guess left."

Fenton took a deep breath and held it. The red light continued to blink. Now his forehead was sweating too. Suddenly he remembered something.

"It rhymes!" he said. "That's it—remember, Max? The technician said something to Miss Ward about punching the numbers in that rhymed."

"Sorry, Fenton," said Max. "I guess I didn't hear that part."

"The *numbers* rhymed?" asked Maggie.

Fenton shook his head. "No, it was the sentence the technician said. I've got it! 'All you have to do is punch one zero one two.' That was it!"

"October twelfth," said Maggie. "That makes sense; it's in the fall."

"Fenton, are you *sure?*" asked Max.

"I think so," said Fenton. "Anyway, here goes." He bit his lip and punched in 1012.

"All *right!*" said Max as the green light switched on.

"Merry Christmas," said Fenton in a whisper. He wiped the sweat off his brow and slowly pushed down the door handle. The door opened.

An eerie red glow from an exit light over the door filled the computer room. They tiptoed through and into the turret.

"We'd better only turn on a couple of these little lights," said Maggie, reaching for one of the desk lamps. "Otherwise it will look like someone's in here from out in the street."

They opened the folding doors to the alcove and hurried over to the historic-materials cabinet.

"What a mess," said Max, looking at the piles of books and papers inside. "Miss Ward should really just scan this stuff into the computer. Then she wouldn't even need this cabinet."

"Let's just hope we can find that journal," said Fenton.

Twenty minutes later, they had finished going through everything in the cabinet and most of the things on the shelves in the alcove. There were books and papers all over the floor, and their hands were coated with dust, but they hadn't found Tipton Van Rensselaer's journal. In fact, they hadn't found anything about the scandal at all.

"Dead end," said Fenton. "All that trouble for nothing."

"I guess we'd better put all this stuff back," said Maggie.

They piled everything back into the cabinet and onto the shelves. Fenton stood up and wiped his hands off on his pants.

"Well, that's that," said Max. "I guess we just have to go back downstairs to the party."

They walked back out into the center area. Fenton shook his head. "I can't give up. Not when I know Mr. Binks is innocent. The thing is, I just can't figure out how it happened."

"Hang on a minute," said Maggie. "Let's look around a little more. Maybe there's some kind of clue somewhere that we overlooked."

"Like what?" said Fenton dejectedly. "It's a little late for fingerprints." Still, he thought, it was worth a try.

"Miss Ward said that the arm was displayed there, in that

storage alcove, right?" Maggie said. "So all we have to do is figure out how somebody else could have gotten in there."

"But you said Miss Ward said Mr. Binks kept the doors locked while he worked, right?" asked Max.

"Right," said Fenton. "In fact, right up until the arm was presented, Mr. Binks had the doors closed. Like this." Fenton closed the two folding doors, sealing off the alcove. "So the alcove was locked up tight." He took his belt off. "Just imagine my belt is the lock." He wrapped it around the two door handles. "And I'm Mr. Binks, giving my lecture out here to the crowd. Then, when I open the doors to let the people in to look, the oviraptor arm has somehow turned into a fake!"

"Pretty weird, " said Max. He looked around. "And I guess these windows in the turret are much too skinny for anyone to have climbed through."

"We're on the fourth floor, too, don't forget," said Maggie.

"Beats me," said Max. Then, suddenly, he brightened. "There is one place we haven't checked for clues, though."

"Where's that?" asked Fenton.

"In the museum's main computer system," said Max. "We can access it from the library computer center."

Fenton looked at Maggie.

"Why not?" she said. "Who knows? Maybe we'll find something."

Fenton doubted there would be much in the computer about the scandal. After all, computers hadn't even been around back then. But he supposed someone could have entered something about it more recently. Besides, he was willing to try anything. He had the feeling that time was running out on their investigation.

"Let's go," he said, and they went out to the computer area.

Twenty minutes later they again had no information, other than finding out for sure that Clara Ward's birthday was on October twelfth, which they already knew. They were about to shut down the computer when they found an electronic file in it called "Presentation Speeches."

"Hey," said Maggie. "Maybe Mr. Binks's lecture is in there."

Max scrolled through the file. "Here it is, 'Binks, Oviraptor,'" he said, bringing it up onto the screen.

They began to read it. It was full of old-fashioned-sounding language, and reading it made Fenton feel almost as if he was back in the early days of the museum, listening to Mr. Binks and waiting for the unveiling of the oviraptor's arm.

Then Fenton had an idea.

"Hey," he said. "I was just thinking. Maybe we should read this out loud. That way we can see exactly how much time there was for something sneaky to have gone on with that arm."

"Okay, go ahead," said Maggie.

"I'll time you," said Max, bringing up a little clock in the corner of the computer screen.

Fenton cleared his throat and began to read, trying to keep an even pace, as he imagined Binks would have done for his lecture.

When he'd finished, the timer said six and a half minutes. They all sat there in silence, thinking.

"Okay," said Fenton, pushing his chair back from the computer. "The way I see it, there are four possible explanations."

8

"Four explanations, huh?" said Max. "Okay, what are they?"

He started to shut down the computer, and Maggie turned her swivel chair toward Fenton.

"Well, first of all, what if there was no hoax at all?" said Fenton. "What if the Smythe Commission made a mistake when they examined the oviraptor arm?"

"You mean maybe the arm wasn't a fake," said Maggie. "The commission just thought it was."

"That's right," said Fenton. "I mean, it didn't look like Binks's work to me, but I guess I could be wrong. After all, he would have made the arm a long time ago. Maybe he wasn't as good at reconstruction then as he is now."

"I guess that's possible," said Max. "But from what Miss Ward said, they examined it pretty thoroughly. It seems kind of strange that they would make a mistake like that."

"Well, how about this, then," said Fenton. "Maybe they made a mistake on purpose. Maybe someone on the Smythe Commission wanted to make Mr. Binks look like a cheat."

"That's possible," said Maggie. "Miss Ward did say that Mr. Smythe, the grandfather, that is, was feuding with the museum director back then. Maybe he wanted to make the museum look bad."

"Or maybe one of the scientists on the Smythe Commission had something against Mr. Binks," added Fenton. "Sometimes scientists have pretty intense rivalries, you know."

"But then who cut the corners out of the floor plans?" said Maggie. "And why?"

"Maybe it was *our* Mr. Smythe," said Max. "Maybe that's what he was doing up here in the library that day. I bet he wouldn't want anyone to find out that his grandfather had made a horrible mistake, since he's so crazy about everyone following the rules."

"Or, even worse, that the Smythe Commission was involved in a fake of its own," said Maggie.

"And we know he doesn't care about the truth, just how things look," said Fenton. "Remember how he wanted Mr. Binks to put up the pteranodon even though its neck bones weren't right?"

"Okay," said Maggie, "that covers two possible explanations. You said there were four. What are the other two?"

"Well, the third explanation," said Fenton, "is that someone did something to the clawed arm. Maybe Mr. Binks didn't even notice it. Or it was switched with a fake one at the last moment. We know he claims that the arm examined by the Smythe Commission wasn't his."

"But how could it have been switched?" said Max.

"And why?" added Maggie.

"If we knew that, we'd probably be able to figure out who did it." said Fenton. "One problem is that we can't even be sure how much of what we've been told is actually true. Someone could be covering something up. Clara Ward, for example."

"Miss Ward?" said Maggie, looking skeptical.

"That's the fourth explanation," Fenton said. "What if the real fraud happened in Mongolia? What if Mr. Binks actually thought he was putting together an authentic oviraptor arm but the parts he'd been sent were phonies—you know, not from the right animal or something. I know Miss Ward seems like a sweet old woman, but maybe we shouldn't be so trusting."

"I suppose so," said Maggie, "After all, she has *her* reputation to protect. Still I don't think she did it."

They sat silently for a moment.

"I guess there's one other possibility that I didn't count," said Fenton with a sigh. "Mr. Binks could have created the fraud after all. Remember, we have no *real* proof that he didn't."

"I guess hiding in the attic all these years could be a sign that he is guilty," said Max.

"But it still doesn't make sense," said Fenton. "I mean, he's so talented. And look at how much he cares about things being accurate."

"Maybe that's just because he got in so much trouble for being *in*accurate way back then," said Maggie, shaking her head.

"And it is true that both he and Tipton Van Rensselaer wanted to become director of exhibits for the museum," said Fenton. "Maybe Mr. Binks thought he had to come up with an amazing exhibit to get the job, so he decided to fake it."

"The trouble is, we just don't have enough clues," said Maggie. She shook her head sadly. "I hate to say this, but we may never know the truth."

"Well," said Max, "we'd better go back downstairs. Your parents are probably starting to wonder where we are, Fenton."

"I doubt it," said Fenton, pushing himself out of his swivel chair. "They usually stay right until the end of the party. But I guess we've done all we can do here anyhow."

"Hey, Fenton, don't forget your belt," said Max. "You left it on the doors to that alcove."

The three of them walked back into the turret. Fenton took his belt off the door handles and put it in his pocket.

"Hey, Max," he said, pushing the alcove doors apart, "want to see the oviraptor arm? It's in here."

But there was no answer. Max and Maggie were both staring into the alcove, with strange, frightened expressions on their faces. He whipped around to see what they were looking at.

There, sitting in a shaft of moonlight on the table in the center of the alcove, was a pair of large, heavy, black leather gloves.

9

"How did those get in there?" asked Max nervously.

"Someone else must have been here," breathed Maggie.

Fenton felt his mouth go dry. What if whoever owned the gloves was still there somehow, watching them?

"But we've been out in the computer area the whole time," he stammered. "That's the only way in."

Max's eyes shifted around the room. "Maybe someone was in the library when we came in. Maybe they hid and went into the alcove while we were out with the computers."

"Fen, your belt," said Maggie. "Was it the way you left it?"

"Exactly," said Fenton.

"So someone *inside* the alcove put the gloves there?" said Max. "That's impossible."

"Unless," said Fenton, thinking.

"Unless what?" said Max.

"Unless there's some kind of secret entrance to this alcove."

"You're right," said Maggie. "Like the box I got for Aunt Margaret! That's got to be it!"

"I guess that means we should look for it," said Max, sounding a little nervous.

"You bet," said Fenton, hurrying into the alcove.

"There's probably some sort of button or catch somewhere," said Maggie, running her fingers along a piece of wood molding.

"Good thinking," said Fenton. He tried touching some of the decorative leaf-shaped woodwork as Max started to feel along the bottom of a row of interlocking vines. "In an old movie I saw on TV once, pushing a flower made a bookcase open."

Maggie checked the wall lamps, and Fenton tried the leaves that were on the other side of the alcove, opposite the first bunch.

"Uh-oh," Max said suddenly, "I think I found something." He was stooping in the corner of the alcove. "There's a little handle under the edge of this bottom piece of carved wood."

"Great, Max," said Fenton. "Try moving it."

They crouched down and waited silently. Suddenly there was a *click* in the wall, and a wood panel swung slowly open. They walked over to it and peered into the darkness beyond.

"There could be someone standing right inside there," Max whispered. It was the quietest whisper Fenton had ever heard.

"We need some light," said Maggie, also whispering very softly. "I'm going to shine the desk lamp in there." She aimed the lamp toward the dark opening. But all that was behind the secret door was a very small room.

"That doesn't make sense," said Maggie. "Why would anyone make a secret panel that only opened up onto a little closet?"

"Maybe it's a sort of safe. They might have stored valuables in here," said Fenton. He thought a moment. "But that still doesn't explain how the gloves got into the alcove."

"Hold on," said Max, looking over Fenton's shoulder. "That wall has vines on it, too. It's the same kind of trim as the one on the secret door. Maybe there's another opening." He crept into the little room and bent down. "Got it," he announced a moment later as another panel swung open.

Maggie stretched the cord of the light as far as it would go.

"Look!" she said. "Stairs!"

Just inside the second panel was a small landing, with an old-fashioned spiral staircase going up. Only the first few steps and the handrail were visible; most of the staircase was in darkness.

"We need a flashlight," said Fenton.

"How about one of the candles back there?" said Maggie.

"Good thinking," said Fenton. He hurried back to Clara Ward's Christmas display, bent down by the little fireplace, and pulled out a candle. He picked up the matches and lit the candle. Then he brought it back to the landing where Max and Maggie were standing. "Here goes," he said.

He started up the stairs, with Maggie and Max close behind him. Around him were wooden planks and dried plaster. He realized that they were seeing the backs of the museum's walls.

As they spiraled around the cast-iron stairs, the walls began to narrow, angling inward.

"We must be going into the roof of the turret," said Fenton.

Finally, they reached a door.

"Are you going to open it?" whispered Max. He didn't sound too sure that they should.

"Of course," said Fenton, turning the handle. The door creaked loudly as it swung open. Beyond it was pitch blackness.

Fenton held the candle ahead of him, and some cobwebs crackled above it. The room had rounded walls and a slanted ceil-

ing, with beams almost low enough to hit their heads. It smelled musty. There were several old packing crates scattered around.

"Look," said Maggie as they went into the room. "Bones!"

Maggie was right. There were dust-covered bones everywhere. Several were scattered on the floor, and there were more on an old set of wooden shelves. A few large ones sat in crates.

"What *is* this place?" said Fenton in astonishment.

"Whatever it is, it gives me the creeps," said Max.

"Come on," said Maggie. "Let's look around."

They picked their way among the crates toward a small, wooden worktable covered with scraps of fossils, tools, and pieces of wire. As they approached it, one of Fenton's feet bumped into something sticking out from underneath.

"Ouch!" he said. He held the candle down and saw what looked like a thigh bone. It was the size of a baseball bat. Nearby, he saw a tiny beam of light coming up from the floor.

"Hey, what's that?" Fenton bent down and saw that the light was coming from a tiny hole in the floor. He put his eye to the hole and found himself looking down into the storage alcove they'd just left. He was directly above the table. "Wow, you guys, you're not going to believe this!" he said excitedly.

"Hold on," said Maggie suddenly. "I heard something."

They froze. Then Fenton heard it, too—footsteps, and they were coming up the stairs. He peered quickly through the peep-hole. The black gloves were no longer on the table in the alcove.

Fenton swallowed nervously. What if it was Mr. Smythe? They were going to be in a lot of trouble if he caught them sneaking around the museum.

91

Then he had an even worse thought. If Mr. Smythe or someone else *was* trying to cover up the truth about the scandal, whoever it was probably knew about the secret stairs to the turret. What if that someone wanted to stop them from uncovering the truth? They might be in danger, and Fenton was sure no one would hear them if they screamed for help from way up there.

The footsteps were getting closer.

Fenton looked around the room wildly. Finally, he motioned for Maggie and Max to hide with him under the worktable. They all crouched down and shuffled back beneath the table as far as they could.

Fenton blew out the candle. The room became completely dark. An instant later the light of a flashlight could be seen.

Fenton held his breath as the footsteps stopped. He could see the light on the ceiling beams and the cobwebs above his head.

The footsteps came into the room and started toward them. Fenton felt himself sweating.

Finally, the footsteps stopped in front of the worktable. Fenton could see two big boots silhouetted against the light next to the bone that he had hit his foot on. Then the light moved and whoever it was crouched down, an arm's length away from them.

Fenton saw a hand reach out toward him. He pulled back against Max and Maggie, his heart pounding.

The hand reached down and grabbed the bone, and Fenton silently took a small breath. The figure stood up and walked slowly back toward the stairs. Soon Fenton heard the footsteps heading down. It was pitch black.

He waited. A few moments went by without a sound.

"Wow," Maggie whispered finally. "That was close."

"It sure was," said Fenton.

The three of them climbed out from under the table.

"Let's get out of here, okay?" said Max. "Where are the matches?"

Fenton reached for his pockets, but he knew before he even checked that he'd left the matches in the library.

"Sorry guys," he said into the darkness, "I didn't bring them."

"How will we find the stairs?" asked Maggie.

"We'll just have to feel our way," said Fenton.

After five minutes of bumping into boxes and tripping on bones, they were back on the stairs.

"Okay," whispered Fenton, "here we are."

He began inching his way down the dark stairs. Soon he could see a faint light coming from the library alcove.

But when they got down to the little room off the alcove behind the first secret panel, Fenton stopped in his tracks, shocked by what he saw. There, directly in front of them, inside the little closetlike room, was a second opening in the paneled wall.

"What's that?" said Maggie, her eyes growing wide.

"It looks like another secret panel," said Max nervously. "Someone else must have opened it."

"Come on," said Fenton excitedly. "Let's see where it goes."

"Do we have to?" asked Max.

"I'll get the matches," said Maggie, running back to the fireplace.

A few moments later, they began circling down the stairs. Fenton could hear dripping water somewhere far below them.

Then, suddenly, he heard a scratching sound.

"What's that?" said Max.

Fenton held up the candle. A rat was sitting several steps below, scratching on the wall. Fenton stamped his foot, and the rat scurried down the stairs.

A moment later they came to another landing with a door. Fenton could see that the stairs continued down, but he paused, looking at the door.

"Do you think we should open this one?" asked Maggie in a whisper.

"Let's not," said Max under his breath. "The glove person could be in there."

Fenton knew Max was right, but he still wanted to know what was beyond the door. Then he had an idea.

"Let's put out the candle," he said quietly. "That way we can crack the door a little bit to peek inside. If someone's in there, they might not notice us in the dark."

Fenton blew the flame out, and they were plunged into darkness again. He could feel Max and Maggie leaning forward as he reached out to put his hand on the doorknob.

Then, suddenly, the door opened, and Fenton felt himself losing his balance. He grabbed for the stair rail with his free hand, but just missed it. He, Max, and Maggie crashed to the landing in a pile.

Fenton looked up, his whole body trembling. Silhouetted in the doorway was a figure. In its hand, held menacingly above its head, was what looked like the thigh bone from the dusty room in the turret.

10

"Come out!" said a man's stern voice. "Or else!"

Terrified, Fenton managed to untangle himself from Maggie and Max. They stood up and inched through the doorway. The figure kept the bone raised, as if ready to strike.

Fenton tried to talk, but his throat was so dry he couldn't. He wasn't sure what he would have said if he'd been able to.

Slowly the man started to lower the bone. Fenton's eyes began to adjust to the light that came in from the street. He saw the man's head jerk back, but his face was still silhouetted by the window behind him.

"Do you know what would happen if I hit you three over your heads with this protoceratops tibia?" the man asked, waving the bone toward them.

The threat made Fenton swallow hard. But there was also something familiar about the man's voice.

"You'd be really dino-*sore*," said the man, starting to chuckle. "That's what!"

Then Fenton realized who it was.

"Jeff!" he shouted. "It's you! What are you doing here?"

"What am *I* doing here?" said Jeff. "You kids are sneaking around at night where you're not supposed to be and you ask *me*, the night guard, what I'm doing here?" Jeff started to chuckle again.

"We thought you were trying to get us," said Fenton.

"I was!" said Jeff, laughing. "That's my job!"

Fenton looked around. They were in a room with wood paneling, like the library had. Something about it was very familiar. Then it hit him. They were in his father's temporary office on the third floor. And on the other side of the door they had just come through was a wood panel carved with the intertwining vine pattern. They had come into the office through another secret passageway to the stairs!

"Oh wow," said Max. "I was scared out of my wits."

"*You* were scared?" said Jeff, between laughs. "Why do you think I picked up that bone? To defend myself!" He switched on the light.

Soon all four of them were laughing and trying to talk at the same time.

"But the secret panels, and the stairs," said Maggie. "How did you know about them?"

"The stairs going *down* from the library aren't secret, at least not to us guards," said Jeff. "Now that other panel and the stairs going up to that room up there in the turret roof *were* secret, though. I had no idea they were there."

"But wait a minute," said Fenton, "where do the stairs go down to from here? Where do you guys come from when you're using them?"

"There's a passageway that runs under the sidewalk to that little guard booth outside," said Jeff. "In case you never noticed,

it's right across the street from the coffee shop. That way you don't have to get cold on your way to get coffee. The other guards showed it to me three years ago. Anyway, sometimes I like to have my coffee in the library alcove. Those big galleries can get lonely and cold at night. The alcove's cozy, especially with the doors closed."

"You mean those were *your* gloves up there, Jeff?" asked Maggie.

"Yep, I forgot them again," said Jeff, shaking his head. "I think I'd better ask my mom to get me some clips like I had when I was a kid, the way I leave those things around. Anyway, when I went back up to get them I saw that second panel open. I was pretty surprised to see it, and then I thought I heard noise, so I followed the stairs up to see what was going on. I couldn't find anything, though, so I went on with my rounds. When I got here to the office I heard noises again, so I decided too check the stairs again."

"We think the stairs and that room at the top of the turret might have had something to do with the Hoax of the Raptor's Claw," said Maggie.

"You mean that thing that happened with old Mr. Binks way back when?" said Jeff.

"Right," said Max. "We think Mr. Binks is innocent. And the way we see it there are four possibilities—"

"I'm not so sure about that anymore," said Fenton.

"Yeah," said Maggie. "I guess there's could be a ton of possibilities now."

"That wasn't what I was thinking," said Fenton. "Now I'm

pretty sure there's only *one* possible explanation."

"One?" said Max, looking surprised.

"Right," said Fenton. "Listen, before I explain, there's something really important I have to do. I'll be back in a few minutes, okay?"

"All right," said Jeff, "but make sure you're back soon. I don't want to have to hear from Mr. Smythe about this."

Fenton hurried out the door and walked quickly down the corridor to the marble stairs, which he climbed two at a time. On the fourth floor he went straight to the door to Mr. Binks's attic office.

He wasn't surprised to see a light under the door. He knocked.

A few seconds went by with no answer. Maybe Mr. Binks was asleep, thought Fenton. His mother had said some people thought he slept there. He knocked again, a little harder.

This time a tired-sounding voice answered.

"Who's there?"

"It's me, Mr. Binks, Fenton Rumplemayer," he said. "Can you come with me for a minute? There's something important I have to tell you about."

11

When Fenton and Mr. Binks arrived back in at the office, Maggie, Max, and Jeff were waiting.

"Well, hello, Mr. B.," said Jeff.

"Oh, hello, Jeff," said Mr. Binks, squinting a little. "And these are Fenton's friends, aren't they? How nice to see you all. But I'm a little confused. What are we all doing here in this office in the middle of the night?"

"That's what I'm starting to wonder," said Jeff.

"It's about the oviraptor's arm," said Fenton. "I think I've solved the mystery."

Mr. Binks gave a start.

"Maybe you'd better sit down, Mr. B.," said Jeff, offering him a chair. "Fenton, why don't you tell us what's on your mind."

"Okay," said Fenton. "Now, we all know that a long time ago the museum sent a bunch of paleontologists to Mongolia. They found amazing fossils, including a dinosaur they thought was trying to rob a nest of eggs."

"Right," said Maggie. "The oviraptor."

"We also know that it was pretty hard to send fossils back in those days," said Fenton. "Some of the fossils didn't even make it back to the museum, or only parts of them did."

"That's right," said Mr. Binks. "And many of the ones that did were terribly mixed up. But reconstructing skeletons back then was very important to the museum's future."

"So important that there were a few people competing at it, right?" said Fenton. "It wasn't even certain who should become the director of exhibits."

Mr. Binks nodded.

"That's true," he said.

"So, only a few pieces of the oviraptor arrived," said Fenton, "but there were enough that Mr. Binks decided that he could try to put together part of it, an arm."

"Well, everyone wanted to see it so badly," said Mr. Binks.

"And right up above us in the library alcove is where you worked on it," said Maggie, "isn't it?"

Mr. Binks had a grim look on his face.

"That's right," he said. "I spent hours in there figuring out that oviraptor's arm. It was so hard, I went a little crazy with it. I wouldn't let anybody in there."

"But someone else *was* there," said Fenton. "Someone you didn't know about. Someone was spying on your work through a hole in the ceiling."

"In the ceiling?" Mr. Binks repeated, looking a little confused.

"That's right," said Fenton. "There's a room up above the library, in the roof of the turret. And there are stairs that go up there from a secret panel in the library, like this one, here."

Fenton tapped on the secret panel. Mr. Binks' eyes grew wide as he stared at the opening.

"In fact," Fenton went on, "it would have been easy for the

visitor to sneak through a secret panel just like this one into your alcove at night to look at what you'd done even more closely. But only a few people knew about the secret doors and the stairs—probably people who had been here when the original museum was built," said Fenton. "Someone was trying to copy Mr. Binks's work. That same person might even have kept some of the Mongolian fossils from getting to Mr. Binks so he could make his own, better, reconstruction."

Jeff shook his head and frowned.

"But the copy wasn't working out so well. The person realized he couldn't compete," Fenton went on. "So when Mr. Binks said he was going to give a lecture before opening his exhibit, this person saw his chance. While Mr. Binks was talking to the crowd, he used the secret stairs to sneak into the alcove, which was still closed behind Mr. Binks. Then he switched the copy of the oviraptor hand that he had made with Mr. Binks's authentic one."

"But who would do something like that?" asked Maggie.

"Only one person could have done it," said Fenton. "Tipton Van Rensselaer, the son of the founder of the original museum, and the person who was using this very office at the time!"

"But why would he do it?" asked Max.

"He had a couple of reasons," said Fenton. "First of all, he and Mr. Binks were both trying to become head of the museum's exhibits. If he could make Mr. Binks look bad, he had a better chance of getting the job."

"I get it," said Max.

"And don't forget," said Maggie. "They also both wanted to marry the same woman, Clara Ward."

Fenton saw Mr. Binks look down at the table at the mention of Miss Ward.

"Tipton Van Rensselaer was also probably upset that his family's original museum had closed," said Fenton. "On top of that, there was the idea that he could be beaten out by someone like you, Mr. Binks, who'd never even had any real training in paleontology."

"I can relate to that," said Jeff. "How many years have I been studying to get my degree?"

"I never realized . . ." Mr. Binks began. But he didn't finish.

"Don't forget, this office we're sitting in right now was once Andrew Van Rensselaer's office, too," said Fenton. "And Tipton was only a boy when the Van Rensselaer Museum of Pre-Historic Life was here. He would have seen the secret panels being constructed."

"And it was his office," said Max, "during the scandal—" he glanced at Mr. Binks, looking a little embarrassed. "I mean, when the oviraptor arms were switched."

"You can call it a scandal," said Mr. Binks. "It was one, though not the one they claimed at the time. Now I can finally understand why the hand that the Smythe Commission showed me wasn't the one I'd reconstructed. When I saw it, I actually thought I might be going crazy. That's one reason I told Clara I no longer wanted to marry her." His voice cracked a little.

"But Tipton wasn't the only one who could have had access to the stairs," said Jeff. "The guards that manned the little guard booth back then must have known about them too."

"They probably did," said Fenton, "but I doubt there was a

paleontologist guard like you on the staff then, Jeff."

"I see what you mean," said Jeff. "They might have been able to get up there, but where would they get a fake oviraptor arm?"

"And they'd have no reason to do it, either," pointed out Maggie.

"And Clara Ward told me that Tipton went to get his journal during Mr. Binks' lecture," said Fenton.

"Which we know took six and a half minutes," said Max.

"And," said Fenton, "I'd guess that was just enough time for him to leave the lecture hall, go down the main stairs to his office, climb up the secret stairs to the turret workroom and get the fake oviraptor arm, go back down to the alcove-"

"And sneak in to substitute his fake work for the arm I'd built!" said Mr. Binks.

"And he'd have been back with Miss Ward just when the commotion of the exhibit opening began," said Maggie, "so she'd hardly even notice he'd been gone."

"Incredible," said Jeff, shaking his head.

Just then, Fenton's eye was caught by a section of paneling on the far wall of the office, behind the desk. Inset into the wall was a small piece of wood carved with intertwining vines.

"Hey, wait a minute," he said, standing up and walking over to the wall.

"What, Fen?" asked Maggie.

"Oh, wow," said Max excitedly, pointing at the wall. "It's the same! The pattern in the wood. It's the same one that was on all the secret panels."

"Hey, look at that," said Jeff.

"Come on, Max," said Fenton, feeling eagerly around the little panel for a catch. "You're good at this."

Maggie gasped. "Do you really think there could be a smaller secret panel there, too?"

Max hurried over. "Only one way to find out," he said.

A moment later there was a *click,* and the little panel swung open to reveal a small cubbyhole in the wall. Inside was a bundle of cloth. Fenton lifted it out and began to unwrap it. But he knew what it was before he even finished removing the cloth.

"Mr. Binks," he said, turning to the old man with a smile, "I think we've found *your* oviraptor hand."

Mr. Binks's face lit up as he took the delicate, well-made reconstruction from Fenton and cradled it in his arms. "Oh, at long last," he said softly. "At long last."

"Wait a minute," said Max, reaching into the cubbyhole. "There's something else in here." He took out a small, leather-bound book. "What's this?"

He began to leaf through it, with Maggie looking over his shoulder.

"It's Tipton's," said Maggie excitedly. "We've found the diary, too!"

12

"Okay, Fen, I guess I'll see you in Morgan," said Maggie. "Tell Max I said goodbye. Oh, and thank your parents again for me."

It was Christmas day, and Fenton was in the kitchen, talking to Maggie on the phone in Connecticut. The Rumplemayers had invited a few people over to the brownstone for a holiday celebration, and the living room was full of guests laughing and chatting.

"I will," said Fenton. "And thank *you* for helping to clear up the mystery of the oviraptor hoax."

"Hey, it was just a normal day of not being a tourist in New York!" said Maggie. "Oh, by the way, Aunt Margaret really liked the antique jewelry box. What did you get?"

"A bunch of good stuff," Fenton answered. "A great new dinosaur book. And my mom got my father and me a video camera. She wants us to tape lots of things in Wyoming for her so she doesn't feel like she's missing out on so much."

"Speaking of missing out, we sure have a lot of things to tell Willy about when we get back," said Maggie.

"That's for sure," agreed Fenton. "Oh, did I tell you? We found the pieces that had been cut out of the floor plans. They were in the back of Tipton's journal."

"I guess that figures," said Maggie. "I wonder what Mr.

Smythe was doing up in the library that day that you and Max saw him, though."

"I asked Miss Ward about that," said Fenton. "She said he rushed up there to make sure she had an official copy of the rules. I guess he wanted to make sure Max and I weren't allowed up there without being supervised by a staff member." He sighed.

"Well, I guess *that* figures too," said Maggie. "Anyway, Fen, I better go. Aunt Margaret's about to serve the goose. I'll see you in a few days. Merry Christmas."

"You, too, Maggie," he answered. "Bye."

Fenton hung up the phone and sat down at the big counter, where Jeff and Max were. Jeff was munching on a cookie, and Max was looking over Tipton Van Rensselaer's journal again.

Fenton's mother came into the kitchen and opened the oven. The room filled with the smell of baking pies.

"You know," said Max, looking up from the journal, "up until Tipton realized he was going to lose the race to make the oviraptor arm, he seems like he was almost a nice guy."

"Yeah," said Jeff. "I guess he just turned desperate."

"And it's rather sad after that," said Mrs. Rumplemayer. "First Tipton thought he'd gotten everything he wanted—the job of exhibits director, Miss Ward's hand in marriage, even his rival, Mr. Binks, banished in shame to the attic."

"But it seems as if he felt guilty," said Jeff. "So guilty that he felt he had to give away everything he thought he'd won."

"Yeah," said Fenton, thinking back to the final journal entries, "so he ran away to a little island."

"It wasn't just running away," said Fenton's mother. "He

thought by working for a doctor in that rough location he might do enough good to undo some of his wrongs."

"Maybe he could have," said Jeff. "But he never owned up to the fraud. That wasn't right."

Just then Fenton's father came toward the kitchen, followed closely by Miss Ward and Mr. Binks.

"Look who's here, everybody," he said.

"Hello, Miss Ward. Hi, Mr. Binks!" said Fenton.

Jeff stood up and gestured for Miss Ward to take his seat.

"I have to be going anyway," he said. "I wanted to stop by to say hello. Thank you for the treats, Mrs. Rumplemayer. Nice seeing you Miss Ward, Mr. B."

"Bye, Jeff," said Fenton. "See you at the museum."

Miss Ward perched herself on the edge of the stool, and Mr. Binks stood behind her.

"Oh," she said to Max, "I see you have Tipton's diary."

"We were just wondering why he didn't tell anyone what he'd done before he went to live on the island," said Fenton.

"Maybe he just couldn't face what would happen if he confessed in person," said Miss Ward. "But I think he expected the diary and the oviraptor arms to be discovered someday. Read what he says in the last part he wrote."

Max turned to the end of the journal.

"'I wish I could turn back the clock to the day the exhibit opened in the turret,'" he read out loud. "'There are two things that you can never get by ruining someone else's life— your self-respect and your honor. I hope that the rest of my life can somehow make up for what I did, and that this journal will someday explain the Hoax of the Raptor's Claw, and clear the innocent.'"

"I guess that meant you, Mr. Binks," said Fenton.

"And you too, Clara," said his mother. "You might never have married him if it hadn't been for the false accusations."

Miss Ward shook her head and gazed at Mr. Binks. Then she took a deep breath and said in a businesslike tone, "Max, what do you usually do Saturday mornings?"

"Nothing special," said Max. "Stuff with my computer."

"I'd like you to help me with *our* new computers," she said, "as a museum volunteer. You're the only one who's ever been able to explain them to me. The director approved the idea. It would only take a couple of hours a week. Would you be interested?"

Max beamed. "You bet I would."

"That's wonderful, Max," said Mrs. Rumplemayer.

"Yeah," said Fenton. He knew Max would have a great time fiddling with the library's computers.

"All right, Max, I'll expect you in the library the first Saturday after New Year's," said Miss Ward. "Oh, and just to make sure we don't get into any trouble with Mr. Smythe, I've brought a volunteer's badge along. You just wear this into the museum when you come."

She reached into her pocketbook and took out a laminated tag with a pin on the back. Written in large green block letters across the top were the words MUSEUM VOLUNTEER.

Mr. Rumplemayer came into the kitchen and put his arm around Fenton's mother. His eyes were shining. Fenton hadn't seen him in such a happy mood since they'd moved to Wyoming.

"So, Mr. Binks," said Mr. Rumplemayer, "I heard the

director's going to offer to give you back your old office in the front of the museum."

Mr. Binks looked amused.

"Yes, it's true," he said. "But I'm not sure I want to move. With the truth known at last, I'm a little proud to be in my cubbyhole."

Miss Ward squeezed his hand and smiled.

"Well, hasn't this turned into a very merry Christmas for all of us?" said Mrs. Rumplemayer. "It's just too bad everyone will be separating soon."

Fenton had been so happy, he'd forgotten that soon he'd be leaving and he wouldn't be seeing Max or Jeff or any of the people at the museum for a long time. He thought about how much he was going to miss his mother. It wouldn't have been a real Christmas without her.

"Well, at least you'll be back with us next summer, Mom," he said, trying to sound cheerful.

"Actually, Fenton, I'm not so sure that the summer will be the next time you see me," said his mother.

"What?" said Fenton. What was his mother talking about? Could it be that she was going to stay in India even longer?

"That's right, son," said Mr. Rumplemayer. "Your mother and I have just been trying to figure something out."

"We thought you might be able to visit me in India during spring vacation," said his mother.

"Really?" said Fenton happily.

This was great news. He was actually going to India! And he'd probably get to help his mother dig for dinosaurs there, too! Fenton didn't know what to be more excited about, all the amazing things she'd told him about, or the new kinds of dinosaur fossils he'd get to see. He couldn't wait until spring vacation.

"Well, this *is* a marvelous Christmas," said Miss Ward, looking around happily.

"What do you say we join the others?" said Mrs. Rumplemayer, nodding toward the living room.

Miss Ward got up from her stool, and she, Mr. Binks, and Fenton's parents headed out toward the other guests.

"Hey, Fenton," said Max as the two of them followed, "I was just thinking. Technically, there are a bunch of places you still can't go in the museum by yourself, right?"

"Yeah," said Fenton a little dejectedly. "Believe me, I'm not looking forward to dodging Mr. Smythe for the rest of vacation."

"Maybe you don't have to," said Max, grinning. "Maybe all you need is an authorized staff person with you."

"Oh great," said Fenton. "You mean follow my parents all over the place? No, thanks."

"No, here," said Max. "Look at this." He handed Fenton his volunteer badge. "Check out what it says."

Fenton looked down at the badge. "'Museum volunteer,'" he read. "I know. So what?"

"Read it again," Max urged. "The whole thing, including the part underneath in smaller letters."

Fenton looked back at the badge.

"'Museum volunteer *staff*'!" he said with a laugh.

"That's right," said Max. "And I, as an official member of the museum volunteer staff, will be glad to supervise you for the rest of the vacation. Just think of it as a Christmas present."

Fenton felt himself grinning from ear to ear.

"That creep Smythe is going to have a fit!" he said.

"I know," said Max, laughing.

In the living room everyone else, Fenton noticed, seemed to be smiling too. His parents were talking happily to their guests, and Miss Ward and Mr. Binks were laughing together in front of the crackling fire.

Fenton looked at them and thought about how long ago it that they had first worked at the museum.

"Hey Max," he said. "You know that history report I told you I had to do? Well, I figured out my topic."

"What's it going to be?" asked Max.

"'The *Real* Hoax of the Raptor's Claw,'" said Fenton.

Mr. Binks must have heard him, because he winked at Fenton before returning to his conversation with Miss Ward.

As Fenton watched the old man talking and laughing, he realized that there was definitely something very different about Mr. Binks now. When Mr. Binks smiled, his smile lit up his whole face. Even his eyes, which had once looked like they would be sad forever, were shining with happiness.

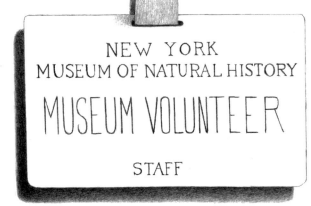

NEW YORK
MUSEUM OF NATURAL HISTORY

MUSEUM VOLUNTEER

STAFF